Popcorn-Eating SQUIRRELS of the World Unite!

To
Stefano

Popcorn-Eating SQUIRRELS of the World Unite!

FOUR GO NUTS FOR POPCORN

MATT DICKINSON

shrine
bell
www.shrinebell.com

PUBLISHER'S NOTE
No squirrels were harmed in the course of writing this book. Several did, however, get rather bad tummy aches.

Popcorn-Eating Squirrels of the World Unite!
Matt Dickinson

First published in 2018 by Shrine Bell, an imprint of Vertebrate Publishing.

shrine bell Shrine Bell
Crescent House, 228 Psalter Lane, Sheffield, S11 8UT, United Kingdom.
www.shrinebell.com

A CIP catalogue record for this book is available from the British Library.

ISBN 978-1-911342-40-3 (Paperback)
ISBN 978-1-911342-41-0 (Ebook)

10 9 8 7 6 5 4 3 2 1

Production by Jane Beagley, Vertebrate Publishing.
www.v-publishing.co.uk

Shrine Bell and Vertebrate Publishing are committed to printing on paper from sustainable sources.

Printed and bound in Scotland by Bell & Bain Ltd.

FOR MY SON
ETHAN

AUTHOR'S CONFESSION

When I was young I really wanted to be a squirrel.

I mean it. I totally did. My friends wanted to be dolphins and man-eating lions and tyrannosaurus rexes and so on, but me? A squirrel. 100%.

I mean, what's not to like? Shiny eyes. Fluffy, silky fur. They zoom about the trees with athletic grace, flying between branches with daredevil casualness.

Most of all I wanted feet that could swivel round. Did you know squirrels' ankles can rotate through 180 degrees? That's how they can climb head first down trees.

Why did I want feet that could swivel backwards? I had a hunch it might help on the football pitch. Or perhaps that it may be handy at the push off for the twenty-five-metre crawl.

And then there's the nuts. It must be cool to be a nut eater, right? There's the macadamias and brazil nuts, the cashews and pistachios and almonds and sweet chestnuts. Like Christmas all year round! Yummy.

Wrong.

Do you know what squirrels *actually* eat? Morning, noon and night?

Acorns.

Nothing but acorns.

Hundreds and thousands of acorns. That's what put me off being a squirrel.

Have you ever tried to eat an acorn? Don't bother! They're *terrible*! Like eating dried-up wallpaper paste. As exciting as a cream cracker that has been hanging around in an Egyptian tomb for 1,001 years.

So I gave up wanting to *be* a squirrel. But I didn't stop *liking* them. And that's how this story began.

CHAPTER 1

MYSTERY IN THE PARK

There were three squirrels living in Blackwater Park. Three young squirrels in the very first years of their lives. Three squirrels who thought they had seen it all.

Ben.

Cassie.

Alfie.

It was true that their short lives had been a rather big adventure. Sometimes too much of an adventure: all three were orphans, their parents lost in a terrible storm.

As wild squirrels they lived on the edge. Every day was like an episode of an extreme survival programme.

Except it was for real.

They'd trembled at thunder bursts and

dodged dodgy dogs. They'd legged it from lightning, bolted from buzzards, and hidden from herons with razor-sharp bills. Cats had crept up on them, trees had been toppled, and the fairground disco had deafened them.

They thought that *nothing* could surprise them.

But they were wrong. Because on this late autumn day, while the three hungry friends were out foraging for buried acorns, something totally unexpected came into view.

Cassie saw it first. Her eyes widened and the fur pricked up on the back of her neck.

'Boys! What's *that?*' she exclaimed. She pointed to the centre of the park where a bizarre-looking creature the size of a monstrously bloated cat dragged itself across the path, moaning loudly.

Alfie and Ben scampered towards it, their noses twitching.

'It's a fat furry monster that can't walk,' Ben squeaked in horror. 'Bloodshot eyes. Yellow fangs.'

'It's grabbing its tummy,' Cassie said, 'and making horrible noises!'

'Alfie happy!' the youngest of the squirrels exclaimed, jumping up and down and dancing a little jig. 'Alfie can play with the big fat furry monster! Yay!'

'Stranger danger, Alfie!' Cassie said sternly.

Ben gave him a strict look.

'Spoilsports!' Alfie tutted, rolling his eyes.

'We should investigate,' Cassie continued. 'But you have to promise you won't get excited, Alfie, OK?'

'I promise,' Alfie said, staring at his friends with his huge brown eyes. 'Naughty Alfie never, ever, ever get even a lickle bit excited ever again.'

The three friends crept cautiously closer as the creature's terrible cries grew ever louder.

'I'm finished!' it gasped. 'It's the terrible pain in ma belly! Will nobody take pity on a pooooooor weeeeee critter?'

'It's not a fat furry monster,' Ben whispered in astonishment. 'It's a fat furry *squirrel* with a Scottish accent!'

Cassie snorted. 'It can't be!'

They crept closer still. The creature saw them and fixed them with a pleading look.

'My guts … ' he called softly. 'My poooor weeee guts are killing me. I need an emergency operation … Get me to a hospital, pals, before it's too late!'

'You're right, Ben!' Cassie exclaimed. 'It is a squirrel! But where has it come from? And what is it doing here?'

CHAPTER 2

CLOSE ENCOUNTERS OF THE FURRY KIND

The three friends stood gawping at
the mysterious new arrival: the biggest,
plumpest, most extraordinary squirrel
they had ever clapped eyes on. A squirrel
with whiskers as thick as steel wire.
A squirrel with glowering brows and
beady eyes and the tuftiest ears ever
seen in squirreldom.

A squirrel wearing a bright yellow
tartan jumper with the words 'NOT
INTERESTED' blazed across the front.

Alfie did a few merry skips to the
stranger and took his paw, a look of
adoration in his eyes.

'Will you be my daddy?' he squeaked
excitedly. 'It'd be great if you're my
daddy! Yay!'

The stranger scowled.

'Alfie!' Cassie pulled Alfie back. 'Don't
you ever listen?'

'He might have fleas!' Ben hissed.

'Never mind being your daddy, laddie, I'm blowing up like a balloon here,' the stranger gasped, his quivering tongue hanging out like a rasher of limp bacon. 'Will you not help out a fellow squirrel in his hour of need?' He clutched pathetically at a handful of weeds, pulling himself forward another few centimetres with a desperate grunt.

'What's your name?' Cassie asked.

The creature's expression soured. 'You don't recognise Salty the squirrel?' he snapped.

'Salteeeee!' Alfie shouted. 'Awesome name!'

'Aye,' the terrifying squirrel said, glaring at Alfie. 'Salty by name, salty by nature, and don't you forget it, laddie.'

His expression suddenly softened and his voice became as sweet as syrup. 'Now, my dearest pals, what can you do to help?'

'Are you sure you haven't just eaten too much?' Cassie asked.

Salty's whiskers began to twitch. 'You're mighty suspicious for a *girl*, aren't you?' he said.

Cassie's eyes flashed.

'Are you saying I'm a wee bit too keen on my grub?' Salty continued. 'Are you saying Salty the squirrel is GREEDY?'

'Yes she is!' Alfie cried. He grabbed hold of Salty's belly and began wobbling it. 'Wibble, wobble, wibble, wobble, wibble! Great big greedy fat boomy bum bum … '

'Look!' Ben yelled, pointing across to the trees. 'It's the megapoodle doggy thing!'

The others whipped round, their hearts hammering as they saw the loose dog running after pigeons.

The megapoodle skidded to a halt and turned towards the squirrels. Slobber dripped from his goofy teeth. Springy hair stuck up in bizarre tufts all over his body.

His eyes narrowed with a look of evil delight.

'He's seen us!' Cassie cried. 'Run!'

CHAPTER 3

CANINE CHAOS

Alfie scampered away in a flash, scattering several panicked pigeons into the air, flapping like crazy.

The megapoodle accelerated, barking wildly, his paws a blur, his eyes wide with excitement.

'I'm stuck on my back, pals!' Salty yelled. His paws bicycled the air, his overstuffed belly wobbling as he wriggled one way then the other.

'Roll me over!' he hissed.

Cassie and Ben grabbed him, grunting as they tipped him back on to all fours.

'The playground!' Cassie yelled. 'Quick as we can!'

Cassie and Ben moved like liquid lightning towards Alfie, already far ahead.

Salty moved like gloopy porridge.
'Doesn't that dog know who I *am?*'
He wheezed.

Little beads of sweat began to collect
in the fur of his ears.

'What kind of freaky dog is it anyway?'
Salty panted. 'Weird-looking beasty.'

'Stop wasting your breath!' Ben scolded.
'Get a move on.'

The dog barked louder, now just seconds
behind the squirrels.

Cassie yelled, 'Throw your jumper!'

'I cannae!' puffed Salty. 'It was knitted
by my dear old ma!'

'Don't be soppy!' she replied.

The dog lunged for Salty's backside,
teeth flashing.

'Whoa!' The enormous squirrel put on
a spurt of speed, slipping off the jumper
and throwing it as he went.

The megapoodle pounced on the
garment, his razor-sharp teeth instantly
ripping it to shreds.

The move won the squirrels a few extra
seconds. Alfie, Ben and Cassie made it
to the playground, rushed around the
roundabout, slalomed past the seesaw
and clambered up the climbing frame.

'Come on, great big pudgy lazy bones!'
Alfie cried to Salty.

'Catch me!' Salty yelled.

He sprang skywards in a desperate
lunge, his jaw clenched tight, his paws
outstretched. Atop the climbing frame,
Cassie and Ben snatched him out of
the air.

The dog raced up, skidded on a slippery
patch of mud and banged into the
frame. The beast slumped to the ground,
momentarily stunned.

High above, Salty was swinging in mid-air, held by Ben and Cassie.

'Don't drop me!' Salty begged. He stared down at the dog, his eyes popping as he saw him stir.

'We're trying our best,' Cassie said through gritted teeth.

The dog's eyes flickered back to life.

Salty fell …

Bounced on the dog's tummy …

… On to a plastic playground frog which was mounted on a huge spring.

As it bent backwards with a squeaky creak, Salty hung on for dear life. Then …

PHHHHTTTTTANG!

The spring shot forward, propelling the unfortunate Salty at high velocity. As he cartwheeled through the air, the calm birdy tweets and distant rumble of traffic were shattered by the loudest and longest and deepest burp that Ben, Cassie and Alfie had ever heard.

BAAAAAAAAAAAAAARP!

'Cool!' Alfie exclaimed. 'He's a flying plumpy whirling burpy stunt squirrel!'

Salty plunged into the middle of the pond and sank out of sight.

CHAPTER 4

POND LIFE

Ten minutes later, after the groggy megapoodle had been chased away by some kind children, the three squirrel friends scurried to the side of the pond.

The surface was deadly calm. Not a ripple could be seen.

'We'll never forget you, Salty!' Alfie called over the water, his little voice cracking as he spoke.

'Never forget me?' hissed a familiar voice from the reeds. 'I should hope not!'

Salty lunged from the shallows, covered in duckweed and green slime.

'It's you!' Ben exclaimed. 'We thought you were fish food.'

'You're alive!' Alfie said. 'Alfie happy!'

Salty emerged on to dry land, shaking

himself and showering the others with pond water.

'Me? Munched by a minnow?' Salty snorted. 'I've got Special Forces survival skills, pal, don't you worry about *me*.'

'*Special Forces?*' Alfie gasped. 'You're my hero!'

Cassie pointed to Salty's tummy. 'Your big belly's gone,' she said. 'It *was* wind after all.'

Salty went red in the face. 'Wind?' he retorted. 'Pish! It was a passing duck who made that dreadful noise.'

'It was you!' Alfie giggled, cartwheeling

across the grass and faking a monster burp as he went. Cassie and Ben snorted with laughter.

'In any case I'm off now,' Salty huffed. 'So I'll bid you all farewell.' Salty waddled away from the pond.

'You sure you don't want to stay?' Cassie called after him. 'We'll share our acorns with you.'

'You can live with us in our tree!' Alfie added. 'If you can fit in the hole.'

'Acorns? Acorns are for losers!' Salty retorted. 'This park's got nothing for Salty, I can tell you, pals.'

The three friends followed him.

'Have you got a better place, then?' Ben asked.

Salty spun around and pointed his finger, dagger-like, at the others. 'You mustn't follow old Salty. Not even if you think he's discovered a secret supply of delicious and wonderful food.'

Everything went quiet for a few seconds.

'A secret supply of delicious and wonderful food?' Cassie said slowly.

'Which doesn't exist,' Salty added, his eyes swivelling shiftily.

'Yum!' Alfie smacked his lips.

Cassie and Ben shared a sharp look.

'Now scram!' Salty said.

The three friends dropped back, watching Salty from a distance. Eventually he reached the trees on the edge of the park and disappeared out of sight.

They heard a car horn blaring out amongst the rumble of traffic.

'Quickly!' Alfie said. He led the way into the trees and the three friends looked around.

'Where is he?' Cassie whispered.

Salty had vanished.

'You don't think he went over the road, do you?' Ben said.

They climbed an advertising billboard and looked out across the thundering traffic at a series of elegant buildings.

The one in the middle had a red neon
sign that read 'REX'.

The squirrels sniffed the air.

'Rex?' Ben said. 'What's a "Rex"?'

'And what's that delicious scent?'
Cassie said.

The friends breathed in deeply, their hungry tummies twisting as the sweet smell zapped into every cell of their bodies.

'More heavenly than hazelnuts!' said Ben, licking his lips.

'More perfect than pecans!' Cassie added.

'Wickeder than walnuts!' Alfie said.

'What IS it?' Ben asked. 'Maybe we should go and see?'

'Let's explore!' shouted Alfie. 'Explore the sweetness, yes!'

'It's too risky,' Cassie said. 'We can't cross the road! Besides, the park is our home.'

Ben sighed. Alfie pouted.

The three friends turned back to the familiar world they knew so well, thinking they would never see Salty again.

They had no idea of the disaster that was about to strike.

CHAPTER 5

CLOUDBURST

That night the rain began. Torrential rain. Freezing wind whipped through the trees and the squirrels' cosy nest was blown away, the leaves and moss scattered by a vicious blast.

The rain continued for a second day and that night the river beside the park burst its banks, swamping everything around.

As dawn broke, the squirrels stared out across a vast lake of floodwater.

'All the nuts we buried …' Cassie cried.

'Our winter supplies,' Ben said quietly.

On the third day, the rain stopped. On the fourth day, the water level fell. The hungry friends came down and sniffed around, finally finding a buried stash of acorns.

Alfie dug one up from the soggy ground and bit into it.

'Bleurgh!' He spat out the waterlogged nut. 'Yucky!'

The acorns were ruined.

Cassie sighed. She scratched half-heartedly at the earth.

'Alfie hungry,' Alfie said. 'Alfie tummy hurts.'

Suddenly the wind changed direction, and Cassie smelled the air.

'The sweetness!' she said, smiling.
'It's back.'

Alfie scampered off to the place where they had last seen Salty.

As Ben and Cassie caught Alfie up, Ben pointed across the road towards the building with the red neon 'REX' sign.

'That's where the smell is coming from,' he said. 'I'll bet my tail on it.'

'Look, there *is* a way across,' Cassie said, staring up at a string stretching from a nearby tree to the roof of the building. It held a banner which fluttered above the middle of the road and read: 'HONK IF YOU WANT TO SAVE THE REX.'

No one was honking.

'We have to try!' Alfie said.

The three friends shot up the tree, stomachs rumbling.

Ben put an experimental paw on the string. It sagged alarmingly.

'It's thin,' he gulped.

'And very wobbly,' Cassie added.

'No probbies!' Alfie protested. 'Easy-peasy.'

Cassie stared at the rushing cars below. They thundered along the road at a crazy speed. The slightest slip from the string would mean being crushed beneath a whizzing wheel.

She shook her head. 'Come away, Alfie,' she said.

Alfie gave Cassie a sulky look but he followed her and Ben.

The three friends sat side by side on a branch of the tree, looking out across the park. As they took in the view, they remembered their adventures of the past.

Many of their memories were happy: the joy of their first spring when the park was alive with flowers, helter-skelter chases up and down the trunks of their favourite trees on sun-kissed summer evenings.

Other places in the park triggered darker thoughts:

The swampy zone where Ben had once

been sucked down into the mud.

The tree struck by lightning, sending Cassie running for her life away from the raging fire when she was just three months old.

The place by the pond where Alfie had been pelted by icy hailstones the size of giant gobstoppers.

So many close calls. So many adventures.

'Oh no!' Ben said, spotting some vehicles arriving. The squirrels groaned at the sight of brightly coloured trucks. It could only mean one thing: another fairground was going to set up in the park.

More disruption. More chaos and noise. And the squirrels were hungrier than ever.

'Maybe Alfie's right,' Cassie sighed. 'This park isn't a good place to live any more. Especially now our food stores have been ruined. We'll starve if we stay here. Perhaps we *should* explore the sweetness.'

Ben nodded.

'Yay!' Alfie cried. 'Let's cross the road. Sweetness or bust!'

CHAPTER 6

THE TIGHTROPE OF DOOM

The three friends went back up to the string and stared out across the road.

The traffic still raced below: cars, trucks, buses, motorbikes. The engine noise was constant, filling the air with roars. Cassie tried to swallow but her mouth was completely dry.

'Here goes for nothing!' Alfie exclaimed.

His paws were a blur as he scurried forward on to the string. Cassie followed, balancing precariously, her tail twitching behind her like a hyperactive snake.

Ben went third.

'It's breaking!' he yelled as he stepped along.

Cassie's eyes widened. Her legs began to tremble. Now she saw the string was

terribly frayed.

'Faster!' Alfie urged, almost halfway now.

Cassie coughed as exhaust fumes filled her throat. Blasts of smoky air buffeted them. She flashed a look at the vans and cars that were speeding past just a few metres below.

'Don't look down!' Ben called.

A rush of wind hit Cassie, flipping her upside down on the string. She gritted her sharp little squirrel teeth and kept on going, paw over paw, commando style, her heart pounding faster than ever before.

Ben gave a shout: 'It's dipping!'

The string began to sag, the weight of the three squirrels dragging it down in the middle.

A double-decker bus roared by underneath, missing Cassie by a tail's length.

'Wheeee!' Alfie sang. 'Great fun!'

'Whoa!' Ben yelled. 'Don't bounce!'

They got to the banner and dug their claws in hard as the sign flapped and bucked about.

'Look out!' screamed Cassie.

A lorry zoomed below.

SWISH!

A metal aerial sliced through the banner like a sword.

Alfie went flying. Cassie grabbed his foot. Then she slipped, just snatching Ben's paw at the last moment. The turbulent air tossed the three squirrels crazily to and fro, Ben's right paw taking the entire load.

'I can't hold on much longer!' Ben cried. His claws ripped through the flimsy cloth of the sign and he slid downwards.

'Swing!' Cassie yelled.

The three squirrels swung left, then right.

Alfie hooked the string with his tail. Cassie got a paw on beside him. Together they pulled Ben up and a heartbeat later they were racing up the string towards the roof of the Rex.

They collapsed on to the tiles.

'Phew!' Ben exclaimed. 'We did it!'

'Told you,' Alfie puffed.

The string went flying as it was snagged by a lorry.

The banner disappeared beneath its

thundering wheels. Their string walkway to the park was destroyed.

'Oh … ' Cassie said quietly. She looked at her two friends, their mouths open in shock. 'That means … erm … we're stuck. We can't go back even if we want to.'

Alfie sniffed the air. 'Sweetness! Stronger than ever.'

'*Sweetness?*' said a familiar Scottish voice. '*SWEETNESS?* What ARE you talking about?'

CHAPTER 7

THE DIRE WARNINGS OF SALTY THE SQUIRREL

The three friends whipped round on the roof.

'I told you not to follow me!' Salty said.

'We had no choice. There's been a flood … ' Cassie began.

Salty took a menacing step towards them.

The young squirrels backed away, their tails down, their ears flat.

'Explain yourselves!'

'We're hungry,' Ben whispered.

'We're exploring the sweetness, that's all,' Cassie mumbled.

'The sweetness … ' Alfie hummed, following his nose and moving towards a hole in the roof.

'Sweetness?' Salty snapped. 'It doesn't exist, d'you hear me? Now go back to where you came from!'

'No sweetness?' Alfie protested. 'Can you not smell the most scrummy, delicious smell in the world? Coming from that hole?'

'No, I cannot,' Salty snapped.

'Alfie take a lickle look anyway!' Alfie decided.

He edged away from Salty and scampered up to the gap in the roof, Ben and Cassie following.

'No!' Salty rushed to the hole with surprising speed, skidding to a stop and carefully wedging in his ample bottom to plug the gap.

A drop of sweat ran down his jowls. His eyes glittered. 'Not so fast my lovelies!' he said. 'You don't know how much danger you're in.'

'Danger?' said Ben.

Salty nodded. 'Aye. Mortal, squirrel-squashing peril!'

'Squirrel-squashing peril?' Cassie whispered. 'How come?'

Salty beckoned them towards him with a sharpened claw. The three friends came in close, eyes wide.

'Inside there,' Salty whispered, 'is *evil*.'

'Evil?' Ben repeated.

'Aye.' Salty licked his lips. 'A squirrel processing plant.'

The three skinny squirrels felt their fur prickle.

'Sq-sq-sq-squirrel processing?' Ben stammered. 'W-w-what's that?'

Salty the squirrel looked around, as if he feared eavesdroppers.

'Squisages,' he said.

The three friends clamped their little paws to their mouths.

'*Squisages?*' Alfie repeated. He began to suck on the end of his tail.

'Aye, laddie, squirrel sausages. Squisages, exported to the five corners of the planet.'

'So why does it say "REX" above the door?' Cassie asked. 'Shouldn't it say "Squirrel Processing Plant"?'

'You're smart,' Salty said, narrowing his eyes. 'Rather *too* smart for a *girl*.'

Cassie bristled but didn't say anything. She needed Salty onside.

'The "REX" thing is just a trick!' Salty continued, throwing up a paw. 'To throw the inspection teams off the scent.'

'Oh, right … ' said Ben.

'That's my mission, you see,' Salty continued, puffing up the fur around his neck importantly. 'Saving other poor wee squirrels by stopping them getting into this terrible, *terrible* place.'

'And they give you lots of nuts for doing that?' Cassie said, frowning. 'I mean, I'm not being rude or anything, but you are rather … well fed.'

'I've always been generously proportioned,' Salty said. He lunged forward, grunting as he tried to pop free from the hole. His eyes began to water. 'It runs in the family.'

The three squirrels retreated two steps.

'You're stuck!' Alfie sniggered. 'Fatty botty stuck in hole!'

Salty puffed. His face went red. He wiggled his backside. 'I'll teach you to spy on old Salty!' Then he woggled his backside. He strained, his eyes bulging. 'I'll teach you to call me … '

Salty clutched at his chest. He gulped at the air.

Meanwhile, Alfie's nose had taken him to another part of the roof.

'There's a different way in!' he cried, sniffing the sweetness. He pushed a loose tile aside. 'We can rescue the poor squirrels inside!'

'Don't you dare!' yelled Salty. 'You don't understand!' He scrabbled against the tiles, his claws scratching furiously on the slate as he tried to get his bottom free.

'Come on!' Alfie called to his friends, jumping in.

'I don't know … ' Ben said as he and Cassie scampered closer. He hopped from one paw to another, hovering on the edge of the hole.

'Alfie's right!' Cassie snapped. 'There's not a moment to lose!'

She pulled Ben inside.

CHAPTER 8

INTO THE SHADOWLAND

Inside the dark cavity of the roof the squirrels paused for a few moments to let their eyes adjust to the gloom until …

BOOM!

An explosion made them jump.

'What's that?' Ben yelped.

Three more thunderous booms followed. The walls vibrated, dust falling from the roof like ghostly veils.

'What are they *doing* to those poor squirrels?' Cassie whispered.

Alfie sneezed as the three squirrels stepped gingerly forward, weaving through stacks of shiny metal canisters. Cobwebs coated the friends in sticky spider silk, making Ben wince. Getting stuck in the swamp as a baby had given him a horror of any type of dirt. He quickly brushed himself clean.

Cassie was exploring the circular cans. 'What do you think these are?' she whispered.

She traced a word on top. 'F I L M,' she said. 'Film.'

Cassie flipped the lid off one of the containers and pulled out a reel of plastic film. Thousands of images were embedded in the strip and Cassie held a section up to a chink of light. She saw a ferocious hairy monster pictured on the old-fashioned movie roll and slowly read

the words: 'Wippy the Werewolf Strikes Again!'

Something shuffled in the shadowy part of the loft.

'What was that?' Ben asked, turning from the film reel.

Ben and Cassie peered into the darkness, the fur bristling on the backs of their heads.

'**YAAAARGH!**' came a yell.

A gigantic werewolf rushed towards them with a blood-curdling cry. Cassie and Ben screamed in terror at its slathering fangs, their little legs a blur as they shot up into the rafters.

'Got you!' Alfie cried.

He pushed the werewolf model to one side, the wheels on its wooden base squeaking. Alfie giggled happily at the sight of his quivering friends.

Cassie and Ben came down, sniffing at the furry pelt of the pretend monster. 'What *is* it?' Ben asked.

'I don't know,' Alfie replied. 'But there are loads of them.'

He led the others to a space beneath the rafters.

Ben and Cassie gasped. There in the shadows lurked dozens of huge models: superheroes and villains, vampires and cybermen. One was a zombie with a chainsaw in its hand.

'I'd like to be a superhero!' Ben exclaimed. 'Half monster, half squirrel. Never afraid of anything ever again!'

'A superhero squirrel?' Cassie said with a smile. 'In your dreams!'

'Alfie already a superhero!' Alfie boasted. 'Alfie not afraid of anything!'

Ben raised an eyebrow. 'Oh no? What about this one, Alfie?' Ben had found a model of a giant hairy yeti, standing on a transparent block of pretend ice.

Alfie flinched as he took in the gigantic snowman. Cassie and Ben knew that Alfie's lucky escape from the hailstones still haunted him.

'N-n-n-not scared of ice,' Alfie
stammered, staring goggle-eyed at the yeti.

'Shh!' Cassie hissed. She could hear an
American voice coming from below them.

'I'm gonna turn you into mincemeat,'
it continued.

A metallic grinding sound rumbled up
through the floor.

'*Mincemeat!*' Cassie whispered. 'They're
processing the squirrels. Come on!'

The three squirrels ran to the speck of
light at the end of the attic.

They got to the spot and found it was
actually a gap in the floor.

'The sweetness!' Ben gasped, sucking in
the delicious smell.

They pushed through the hole … into
a strangely shaped chamber of chiselled
stone.

'Yuck!' Alfie said, looking down at his
paws. 'Alfie standing on a tongue!'

CHAPTER 9

THE SWEETNESS BECKONS

'A tongue! Don't be silly,' Cassie said.

She looked down, frowning. Alfie was right. The floor did seem to be carved into the shape of a tongue.

Long, slithery and evil.

'We're in a mouth!' Ben said. 'What's going on?'

The three squirrels crept forward, blinking in surprise as they looked down on row after row of plush red seats, some filled with people.

Cassie could see now that they were peeping from the mouth of a stone gargoyle – a griffin with a wickedly sharp beak. She spotted other fantastical monsters occupying the other three corners of the auditorium: an ogre, a serpent and a gorgon with snakes for hair.

'Where are the processing machines?' Cassie whispered. 'What are those people doing?'

'Wow!' Alfie gasped, noticing the huge bright screen at one end of the otherwise dark room. 'Kung fu kangaroos!'

The squirrels watched as four kangaroo superheroes used their martial art skills to fight squid-like aliens. Behind them a whole forest was in flames, the trees crackling as they burned.

'Fire,' Cassie whispered in a quavering voice, 'like the night of the lightning tree.' She shrank backwards, into the shadows.

'Salty has been fibbing,' Ben said with a frown. 'This building is not a squirrel processing plant. It's … it's a place for humans to watch stories.'

He looked around at the families below them, and groups of older children in twos and threes.

'The sweetness!' Ben sang. 'We're close.

It's here.'

'Really?' Cassie said. She crawled forward and looked down.

'The children are eating … ' Ben whispered.

'White stuff!' Alfie finished.

Every few seconds a little white speck of sweetness flew through the air, touching down on the head of an unsuspecting child.

The target would whip around, then zap

a piece of sweetness at the attacker in revenge.

'They're throwing it at each other!' Ben said in surprise.

'That boy at the front is flicking his at the screen,' Cassie added.

The squirrels watched as an adult next to him pulled the carton of sweet stuff away.

Meanwhile, on the screen, the superhero kangaroos had won their battle. All that was left of their alien enemies was little puddles of sludgy grey goo. Music started and lines of writing moved up the screen.

The lights flashed on, making the squirrels blink. The spectators walked out, chatting happily about the film. Within minutes, the room was empty.

'Sweetness everywhere!' Alfie said in amazement. 'Spilled all over.'

'They're the messiest humans ever,' Cassie agreed, her tummy rumbling. 'Let's take a closer look.'

The squirrels leapt for the nearest curtain, clinging on to the velvet drape and shimmying down to the floor.

They darted cautiously across the aisle and into the seat rows where the little white pieces of sweetness were scattered all over the floor.

'Here goes!' Alfie exclaimed, and chomped a fluffy piece of the sweet stuff, his eyes widening. Cassie and Ben watched him anxiously. Then a smile of pure delight filled Alfie's face.

'Sensaaaaaaational!' he said.

He thrust one piece after another into his mouth, his cheeks soon bulging.

Cassie nibbled a bit. Ben did the same.

'Oh,' she said.

'Wow!' said Ben.

Cassie picked up a carton and read it out loud.

'P O P C O R N … Popcorn,' she said. 'That's what the sweetness is. It's *popcorn*!'

CHAPTER 10

THE TASTE OF HEAVEN!

'Popcorn!' Ben shouted, throwing his paws aloft. He scooped up pawfuls of the crispy white snack from the floor and ate it with delight.

'Popcorn!' Alfie repeated. 'It even *sounds* delicious! Poppy and corny and yummy and wow!'

'We're saved!' Cassie exclaimed. 'We can live here for ever, and never be short of food!'

Alfie was scooting forward on his tummy, munching down one fluffy white piece of popcorn after another, like a super-powered squirrel-based vacuum cleaner.

'This one's half full!' Beaming, Ben upended the carton over his head, showering himself with a glorious cascade.

'I get it!' Cassie said. She had been studying the cartons. 'There are four flavours. Butter. Caramel. Salty. Plain.'

'Butter, caramel, salty, plain,' Alfie sang, gobbling down a piece of popcorn with each word as he worked his way along an aisle. 'Butter, caramel, salty, plain, butter, caramel, salty, plain, butter, caramel, salty …'

He bumped into two huge and hairy paws.

'Sweaty feet,' he squeaked.

'Sweaty feet?' Ben asked. 'Who in the world would buy a carton of … ' Ben poked his head over the seats and his jaw dropped. 'Oh.'

There were two new arrivals.

A man with a scowling face and a beard that looked like it might be hiding all manner of bugs and beetles.

And Salty the squirrel. The owner of the sweaty feet.

'Enough's enough, my wee lovelies,'

Salty said quietly. 'You can stop eating *my* popcorn now.'

'*Your* popcorn?' Ben questioned, putting his paws on his hips.

'Aye,' Salty said, grinning. 'All mine, isn't that right, Nigel?'

The man smiled. 'Yes, Salty, that's right.'

'You lied to us!' Cassie said. 'There's no squirrel processing plant here.'

'Aye.' Salty crammed a pawful of popcorn into his mouth. 'Some squirrels *do* lie! Now get over it, *girly*!'

Cassie glared back. 'You just wanted to keep all this popcorn for yourself!' she said. 'You're the most selfish squirrel we've ever met!'

'Salty should share it,' Alfie said, shaking his head. 'And Alfie doesn't want you to be his daddy any more!' He picked up a piece of popcorn and raised it to his mouth.

Salty leapt forward, batting the popcorn out of Alfie's paw.

'Let me tell you how things are,'
Salty said. 'Me and Nigel here have got
ourselves a wee agreement, haven't we,
Nigel?'

'That's right, Salty.'

'Nigel's in charge of cleaning this place
after every screening, aren't you, Nigel?'

'That's right, Salty.'

'But you're a wee bit lazy, Nigel, would
that be fair to say?'

'That's right, Salty.'

'So Nigel puts his feet up and has a
nice cup of tea and I do the business in
here out of the kindness of my wee heart,
eating *every* last piece of popcorn, after
every single movie.'

'No wonder you're so lardy!' Ben said.

'Now, get lost,' Nigel growled at the
three friends. 'Or I'll set Donny on you!'

Salty turned to Nigel, his brow furrowed.
'Donny?' he said. 'Who's Donny?'

'Didn't I tell you?' Nigel replied.
'I found a stray dog running around in

the park. Funny-looking creature – I think
he's a doberdoodle. Donny! Here, boy!'

He gave a shrill whistle and a
tufty-haired dog ran eagerly into the
auditorium.

The four squirrels stared in horror at the new arrival.

'It's the d-d-d-dog from the park!' Ben stammered.

Donny the doberdoodle began to snarl, his eyes glaring with pure hatred as he saw the squirrels.

Nigel grabbed his scruff. 'Steady boy!' he said, glancing nervously at the furious dog. 'Control yourself or I'll put you back in your cage.'

The sound of voices caused them to swivel round.

Footsteps were approaching the auditorium.

The door opened.

The four squirrels dashed for the safety of a curtain, hiding themselves behind it.

CHAPTER 11

ROSALBA
OF THE REX

'The manager!' Nigel gasped. A portly man waddled into the auditorium, his shiny suit glimmering in the spotlights.

With him was a lady wearing a fixed smile and a faded green ballgown and cape. She looked as if she had just come from an unsuccessful audition for a role in a Christmas panto.

'May I introduce *Rosalba*!' the manager gushed. 'The new owner of the Rex.'

Nigel grunted and offered a grubby hand.

'This is Nigel the … erm … cleaning chap, and his guard dog, Donny.'

Rosalba glanced at Nigel's stained fingers, stared in bemusement at Donny for a second then rushed past, spinning gaily round and round in the aisle, the gigantic pearls around her neck clacking sharply. 'I have bought myself a little slice of cinema history!' she trilled.

'The romance of the silver screen,' the manager agreed, 'has indeed seeped into the very fabric of the place.' He leant casually against the wall, placing his hand over a particularly sinister-looking stain in the velveteen cladding.

'I was once an actress myself,' Rosalba said, ending her pirouettes and staring briefly at her wrinkled reflection in a tarnished mirror. 'I could have graced every cinema screen on the planet if only those incompetent directors had recognised my extraordinary talent.'

She licked a bony finger and smoothed a spindly eyebrow back into shape.

'The world of entertainment was cheated,' the manager said.

Rosalba pulled a publicity brochure from her handbag. 'There are going to be some changes,' she announced. 'That popcorn machine you've got out there in the foyer is rubbish!'

Nigel and the manager came closer to the brochure, whistling as they studied the glossy photos.

'The Pop-O-Matic 3000,' the manager said in awe. 'The Rolls-Royce of the popcorn-making world.'

'The very best!' Nigel agreed.

'The biggest popcorn machine in the world!' Rosalba chirruped. 'I've ordered one – and it's coming later today!'

Rosalba folded the brochure away, then picked at a hole in a seat cover with a chipped fingernail. Her lips pouted slightly and she frowned as puffs of stuffing spewed out from the hole.

'Tatty!' she snapped. She crossed to the screen and scraped off a few flecks of dried matter. 'Dirty!'

She stepped towards the toilet door, placed a powdered hand on the handle,

then sniffed, froze for a moment and
turned away.

'We're talking *total* renovation,' she said
firmly.

Rosalba reached for the nearest curtain, pulling it up to wipe her hand. The four squirrels hiding behind it clung to the fabric so they wouldn't be seen.

'Yes!' The manager smoothed his hair across his shiny scalp. 'Total renovation. That's what I've been saying for almost twenty years.'

Rosalba dropped the curtain. Salty tumbled out on to the floor, then dashed back for cover.

Rosalba shrieked. 'A rat!' she exclaimed, stumbling backwards. 'I saw a rat!'

'Surely not,' the manager coughed. 'Most unlikely.'

He flashed a scorching look at Nigel and Donny. Nigel's cheeks turned red. A nervous tick twitched at the corner of his mouth.

'I'm sure of it!' she raged. 'A scabby rat! A big fat thing! The ugliest rodent I ever saw in my *life*!'

Behind the curtain, Alfie sniggered.

He pointed at Salty, whispering, 'Scabby rat! Scabby rat!'

Rosalba moved in closer to Nigel, her lustrous crimson lips centimetres away from the cleaning man's bulbous, blotchy nose.

'I want it caught,' Rosalba hissed. 'And *disposed* of.'

'Yes m-m-m-ma'am,' Nigel stammered.

'Immediately. Or there will be serious implications for you and your … ' She gave Donny a withering look. 'Thing.'

Rosalba tossed her silken cape over her shoulder and swept from the room.

'You heard her,' the manager snapped at Nigel, scurrying after his new boss.

CHAPTER 12

DOBERDOODLE DANGER

The squirrels emerged from their hiding place, keeping a safe distance from Donny.

The doberdoodle gave them the evil eye as Nigel held him by the scruff of his neck.

'We're in big trouble now,' Ben said, his voice trembling.

Salty snorted. 'Trouble? Pish! She thinks that Nigel will obey her, but I know better. You see Nigel is my *pal*, isn't that right, Nigel?'

The auditorium went deathly quiet for a few seconds.

'That's *wrong*, Salty,' he said.

Salty went pale. 'Wr-wr-wrong?' he stammered. 'How do you mean?'

'This is a dog-eat-dog world,' Nigel said. 'Or should I say dog-eat-squirrel.'

Nigel released his grip on Donny. 'Attack!'

The doberdoodle lunged. The squirrels scattered.

'Go for it, boy!' Nigel yelled. 'Get Salty! He's the one she's seen. I'll go and get your travelling cage.'

Ben shot up the wall. Cassie sprinted between two rows of seats. Donny picked Cassie out with a delighted yelp, his razor-sharp teeth snapping. Cassie could feel the heat of his evil breath puffing against her back.

'Not her! I said get the gobby one!'
Nigel called.

Donny switched to Salty, sweat flying as
he shot down the aisle.

'That's right,' Salty puffed, his tongue
hanging out. 'Pick on the weakest link,
why don't you?'

Donny glanced to his left. Something
had caught his eye. Alfie had placed a
popcorn carton over his head and was
standing, quivering, on a seat, muttering
over and over.

'Can't see Alfie. Alfie invisible. Can't see
Alfie … '

Donny spun and took a mighty leap. His jaws opened wide.

'Alfie!' Ben screamed. He grabbed his young friend by the scruff, and yanked him back as Donny snapped at thin air. Ben pushed Alfie through a doorway, into a room where a huge roll of movie film was being rewound on to a spinning table.

'Like a zoomy snake!' Alfie gasped.

The thin band of film was moving at high speed, looping this way and that across a system of little wheels.

Cassie came into the projection room a second later, with Salty panting at the rear.

'Up here!' Ben said.

He led the way up the moving strip of film. It was hard work – like trying to run the wrong way up an escalator.

Donny ran in and leapt on to the spinning turntable, his legs a blur.

For a few crazy seconds all five creatures sprinted at high speed, going precisely

nowhere, like hamsters running inside
a wheel.

Then Cassie jumped.

'Ha!' she cried, hitting a lever and
bringing the projector rewind to a sudden
jarring halt. Donny was bundled on to the
floor, jumbled in a twisty straightjacket of
plastic film.

'So long, suckers!' Salty exclaimed. He
dashed out of the room and scrabbled up
a curtain.

Donny bit himself free and gambolled
out in hot pursuit. Alfie, Ben and Cassie
followed on, hiding behind some seats in
the auditorium as they watched the chase.

Salty was halfway up the curtain
when Donny shook the cloth with his
teeth. The overweight squirrel bucked
awkwardly up and down.

'Give me a break, pal,' Salty begged,
scrambling higher. The velvet ripped as
his claws dug in. Donny climbed after
him, clamping his jaws on the fabric and

rising up in a series of lunging bites.

'I can't watch!' Cassie muttered.

Alfie covered his face.

Salty took a desperate jump for the gargoyle above him.

Donny swiped a paw, clipping Salty.

'No!' Salty cried. He missed the gargoyle by a claw's length and spun towards the ground.

'Gotcha!' Nigel said. He snatched Salty out of the air, thrust him into a cage and slammed the door.

CLICK!

Nigel snapped the hefty padlock shut.

The exhausted Donny flipped down from the curtain and got an affectionate pat from his master.

'Well done, lad,' Nigel said. 'We've got the ringleader and the others will be running for their lives if they know what's good for them. I'll have a cup of tea and then we'll take this pest down to the rubbish dump … '

Donny panted with pleasure.

'Let's see how he gets on with the rats.'

CHAPTER 13

SALTY GETS IN TOUCH WITH HIS SWEET SIDE

The squirrels exchanged glances, then watched from their hiding place as Nigel and his hound quit the auditorium, leaving the cage on the floor.

All was quiet.

'Pals?' came a quavering voice. 'Are you there, my old chums?'

Ben looked at Cassie, raising his eyebrows in two mini arches.

'It's your old pal, Salty,' came the voice again, this time sounding close to tears, 'reaching out to his true mates, his good old buddies, in his time of need.'

'Would that be the same Salty,' Ben called out sternly, 'who a couple of minutes ago was abandoning us with a rabid doberdoodle and shouting, "So long, suckers!"?'

There was a lengthy silence.

'I'm taking medication,' Salty whined, 'for my poor wee joints. It's the pills that turn me sour, old pals. I'm a different person deep down. As sweet-natured a squirrel as you'll ever meet.'

Alfie strolled down the aisle, picking up pieces of popcorn as he went and pausing just a tail's length from the bars of the cage.

'Salty doesn't mind?' he said. He stuffed the popcorn into his mouth and chewed them with a grin.

'Mind?' Salty choked. 'There's nothing old Salty likes more than seeing his pals enjoying a good feed.'

Cassie and Ben emerged into the aisle and also began to eat.

'So that thing you said,' Cassie asked between mouthfuls, 'about what would happen if we touched even a single piece of popcorn?' She chomped on a good mouthful.

'That!' Salty laughed manically as he clutched at the bars of the cage. 'Old Salty was having a wee joke.' Salty shook the bars, rattling the lock. It didn't budge. Drips of sweat ran down his ears.

'The clock is ticking, pals,' he said, his voice trembling. 'We only have the time it takes to make a cup of tea. Have you come up with a rescue plan for old Salty?'

'Rescue plan?' Ben said. 'Nope.'

'But you heard what Nigel said.' Salty gulped. 'About … about the … r-r-r-rats at the r-r-r-r-rubbish dump?' Salty's left eye began to twitch. 'I need action, pals! What are you all going to do to get me out?'

Cassie approached the cage. She took the padlock in her paw and gave it a good tug.

'There might be a way,' she said thoughtfully. 'But we need to negotiate first.'

'Negotiate?' Salty snorted. 'With a *girl*?'

'We share the popcorn between us,' Cassie interrupted through gritted teeth. 'Split four ways.'

'For ever,' Alfie added. 'Yay!'

'For ever?' Salty snorted. 'But how will poor old Salty survive on just a quarter of his ration?'

'"Poor old Salty" will be better off,' Cassie said sternly. 'You might even slim down to a healthier weight.'

'Agree,' Ben said, 'or it's living with the

rats for you.'

Salty ground his teeth together with
a horrible crunching sound.

'All right!' he snapped, finally. 'I agree.
Now get me out of this nightmare!'

'Shake on it,' Cassie insisted. Salty poked
his paw out and he and Cassie shook.

Cassie leapt into action. 'Ben, Alfie!
Follow me!'

Cassie climbed the curtains in a flash,
her two friends following behind.
They jumped for the griffin gargoyle,
scampering through the mouth and up
into the attic.

Ben gasped. The zombie model was
right in front of them.

'It's not the zombie we want,' Cassie
explained. 'It's the chainsaw!'

The three squirrels clambered up and
wrestled the chainsaw free, sharing the
weight between them to get it to the
ground.

Alfie tested the cutting teeth with his

paw. 'It's really sharp!' he said.

'It's not going to whizz round and round though,' Ben said. 'It's just a pretend one.'

Cassie smiled mischievously. 'You don't know the plan yet,' she said. 'Our friend Salty is in for the ride of his life.'

CHAPTER 14

SALTY GOES FOR A LITTLE SPIN

Cassie's cunning plan rolled into action, and the squirrels lowered the chainsaw into the auditorium on a piece of rope they'd found coiled in a dark corner of the attic.

Salty gulped as he saw the power tool swinging down, the razor-sharp teeth glinting in the spotlights.

'What're you planning, pals?' Salty asked, his voice high.

'You just relax,' Cassie said soothingly. 'Leave everything to us.'

'Relax?' Salty snorted. 'I'll put my feet up, shall I? Never mind the fact that I'm about to be sliced in two by a chainsaw and then taken to the rubbish dump!

Och aye, that's very relaxing, that is!'

He paced up and down in the cage, his tail jerking from side to side.

'Stage one,' Cassie announced. 'We have to get this cage into the projection room at the back.'

The three friends dragged the cage up the aisle, Salty muttering all the way. They made it to the room and kicked reels of film aside to get some space.

'Now comes the heavy part,' Cassie said. 'Get him on to the rewind table.'

'The rewind table?' Salty said. 'What the … ?'

'Let's do it,' Ben said. 'One, two, *three*!'

The three squirrels lifted the cage, puffing and straining and stretching upwards to reach the table.

'You weigh a ton!' Alfie said.

The cage slid on to the circular rewind table.

'Well?' Salty said. 'What next, Mrs Einstein?'

'Get the chainsaw!' Cassie told Alfie and Ben. The two squirrels dashed out as she began to search some nearby drawers. 'Eureka!' she cried. Cassie pulled out a big roll of parcel tape as the others came back in with the chainsaw.

She ripped the end free, handing it to Ben and biting off a length.

'Stick the cage to the table,' Cassie said. She bit off strip after strip of tape. Two minutes later they had the cage taped firmly in place, the metal bars lined up

with the edge of the rewind table.

Cassie pulled the lever. 'Spin time!' she cried.

The table began to turn, rapidly picking up speed.

'Whoa!' Salty gasped, his feet doing a little dance as he tried to keep his balance.

'Now grab the chainsaw,' Cassie instructed. 'Hold it here!'

Ben and Alfie helped Cassie to raise it up high.

ZING! The metal bars of Salty's cage rasped against the teeth. Salty gasped.

ZING! Another rotation. A spark flew off.

'Faster!' Alfie said.

Ben pulled the rewind lever down an extra notch. The table accelerated. Salty was starting to go green as he whizzed around.

'Erm, pals. I'm getting a wee bitty sick in here!'

ZING!
ZING!

Bigger sparks began to fly. Salty grabbed the bars at the back of the cage, his cheeks wobbling as he was hit by the G-force.

'It feels as if my brains are coming out of my ears!' Salty cried.

'It's working!' Cassie yelled triumphantly.

'Aim for the padlock!' Ben said.

The three friends strengthened their grip on the chainsaw.

'Maximum speed!' Cassie cried.

Ben stuck out his foot and nudged the lever down to level ten. The cage was whirring so fast that Salty was just a furry blur.

Then …

'Aaaaargh!' Salty cried.

PING!

The padlock disintegrated in a shower of shrapnel.

Ben hit the stop switch. The table slowed.

'Salty?' Cassie said.

An oily cloud of smoke wafted up from

the guts of the rotating table. A deathly groan came from within the cage. The door swung open and Salty emerged, swaying unsteadily from side to side, his fur swept back as if he'd been standing in a hurricane. He clutched his belly, his eyes rolling.

'Never, ever do that again,' he muttered, then toppled forward into a wastepaper bin.

Voices came from the auditorium. Cassie jumped up to the projection window.

'They're coming back,' she said. 'Salty! Where can we go?'

CHAPTER 15

MARCHING ORDERS

The friends pulled the groggy squirrel out of the bin.

'Up there,' Salty said weakly. He scrabbled clumsily for the top of a cupboard. 'We can get out this way.'

Salty squeezed through a hole in the wall where an air conditioning unit had been badly fitted. Ben, Cassie and Alfie followed, peeking back down through the gap as Rosalba and the others entered the projection room.

'What on earth … ?' Nigel stared dumbly at the empty cage. 'He was in there, I swear!'

'Idiot!' Rosalba hissed. 'We can't have vermin running willy-nilly all over the cinema.'

'I'm s-s-s-sorry,' Nigel stammered.
'I don't know how he—'

'You're fired!' Rosalba shrieked, pointing to the door. 'And you can take that mangy mutt with you.'

'But—'

'I gave you a simple task and you failed. Now go. And don't come back.'

Nigel flushed bright red, then looked to the manager. 'Cyril?' he whispered.

The manager shook his head and looked at the floor.

Nigel walked slowly from the room, taking Donny with him.

'This vermin problem needs sorting IMMEDIATELY!' Rosalba snapped, jabbing at the manager's chin with her finger. 'Or you'll be out on your ear as well.'

The manager mopped at the moisture on his brow with a grubby handkerchief. 'I've got a friend who runs the Roxy,' he said. 'He got his vermin wiped out in twenty-four hours by this extermination

team. He said they're oddball, bit of a
rum bunch, but they get results.'

'I don't care if they're oddball,' Rosalba
said. 'I don't care if they're as rum as a
pirate's breakfast. I don't care if they're
a bunch of knife-wielding ninja honey
badgers from Bognor Regis, as long as
they get these horrible creatures OUT
of my cinema.'

The four squirrels had heard enough.
They retreated to the attic and huddled
together for a conference.

'What are we going to do?' Cassie moaned. 'That Rosalba woman is going to get rid of us one way or the other.'

'But we can't run away,' Ben said. 'We've got food for life with all this popcorn.'

'Alfie stay,' Alfie added. 'Popcorn for ever!'

'Yes,' Ben said. 'Whatever evil plans those humans come up with, we have to be smarter. Stay one step ahead.'

The attic trapdoor creaked. Light flooded in as it pushed up. The squirrels scrambled into a hidden corner.

'This is the final stop on our little tour,' the manager said. 'The storage area.'

'Storage area?' Rosalba snorted as she looked around. 'It's a dump. And what on earth are these ghastly monsters?' she asked, pulling out some of the movie figures from the shadows.

'Promotional models for the films,' Cyril said. '*Little Bo Creep. Helldragon. The Abominable Snowman.* Good film, that.'

'Get rid of them!' Rosalba said. 'They give me the heebie-jeebies.'

'Yes, ma'am.'

A mobile began to ring.

'My phone,' the manager said. He snapped it open, listened for a few moments. 'The popcorn machine is here,' he told Rosalba.

'Oh, goodie!' Rosalba clapped her hands together then climbed down the attic steps, the manager behind her.

'Come with me,' Salty said. 'We can't miss this.'

The squirrels followed Salty, down the steps and along the curtain rail, crawling into a gap in the ceiling.

They came – just in time – to a spying place above the foyer.

CHAPTER 16

THE POPCORN MACHINE OF THE GODS

The squirrels watched as five sweating delivery men manhandled a massive object into the foyer.

Hot on the heels of the workers came a tall, extremely handsome man, with a slick head of inky black hair and a deep and rather orange tan. He was a snappy dresser – so snappy that it wouldn't be surprising if mousetraps fell from his trouser legs with every step.

'Greetings!' the man drawled. The words oozed from his lips like treacle. 'Greetings to you all, my dearest popcorn aficionados!'

He raised Rosalba's hand to his lips,

fixing her with his melty brown eyes.

'I've always had a soft spot for ladies of a certain age!' he murmured huskily.

'What a *gent*!' Rosalba croaked, her neck flushing scarlet. 'And *what* a machine!'

'I recognise you,' Cyril said to the man, a slight tone of suspicion in his voice. 'Didn't you used to be that children's magician? Fan … Fan … whatshisname?'

'Fandango!' the man said, bowing so deeply his black wig flopped forward to reveal a shiny bald patch atop his head.

'That's it.' The manager frowned. 'There was that unfortunate incident with the rabbit … I read about it in the paper. The court case and so on—'

'Yes, yes!' Fandango said hurriedly, patting his wig back into place. 'Those days are over. We've all moved on. Including the rabbit. He's doing perfectly well … so far as I know.'

Rosalba took hold of the dust sheet that covered the machine. 'May I?' she enquired.

'Normally *I* am the one to unveil the machine,' Fandango said testily. 'After all, I, *Fandango*, am the one who—'

Rosalba yanked the dust sheet away.

'Wowee!' Alfie breathed.

'The popcorn machine of our dreams,' Salty gasped.

'The Pop-O-Matic 3000,' Rosalba whispered in awe. 'This will bring the crowds back to the Rex!'

The machine was indeed wondrous, fitted with so many dials, knobs and pressure gauges it could almost have passed for a spaceship.

The top bit, the popcorn creation zone itself, was extraordinarily huge, a polished metal container with hundreds of buttons and dials, big enough to fit several fully grown men inside.

'Spec … tacular!' Cyril whistled.

'All my own work,' Fandango crowed. 'The first in a series of inventions that will change the world!'

'Plug her in,' Rosalba said eagerly. 'Give us a demo.'

'Certainly,' Fandango agreed. 'Then you'll see why this is my bestselling invention. We're even putting one on that new cruise ship they're launching down at the docks.'

The delivery men rolled massive barrels of unexploded popcorn into the foyer.

'How exciting!' Rosalba shrieked.

One of the delivery men handed Fandango a small set of scales. He filled a bucket with unexploded popcorn and checked its weight. 'Got to be a teensy-weensy bit careful,' he said with a slightly nervous chuckle. 'I haven't fully tested the overload system.'

He plucked out a single kernel and flicked it back into the barrel. 'Five kilos exactly!' he said. 'Not a microgram more.'

He poured the popcorn kernels into the machine.

'Inferior machines use hot oil,' Fandango said. 'That's how you get uneven popping, hard bits, broken teeth, etcetera.'

'Nasty!' Rosalba shuddered, pausing to readjust her dentures. 'We don't want THAT at the Rex.'

'Whereas I borrowed a technique from the Song dynasty of China,' Fandango continued. 'Then I cleverly improved it with a brand-new neutron capacitor that generates a frequency of popcorn-specific wave which takes the gelatinous—'

'Yes, yes!' Rosalba snapped. 'That gobbledygook is all very well, but let's just make some popcorn, shall we?'

Fandango gave her a flinty look. 'Very well,' he said.

He flipped a switch. The room filled with a loud hum.

Lights flashed. The machine shook as the pressure inside began to build.

'It's incredible!' Rosalba sang.

Then a countdown screen flickered to

life, along with a deep male voice which announced: 'Ten. Nine. Eight. Seven. Six. Five. Four. Three. Two. One.'

Up in their spying place, the squirrels looked at each other, their eyes boggling with excitement. There was a moment's pause. Then …

CHAPTER 17

POPTASTIC DEVELOPMENTS

The Pop-O-Matic 3000 rocked violently as the corn exploded. The massive container at the top was suddenly packed to the brim with delicious, steaming-hot popcorn.

'Let's taste it!' Rosalba said. She shoved the lid aside and grabbed a handful.

The squirrels groaned as the scrumptious scent reached their noses.

'Great Scott!,' Cyril said. 'It's the best popcorn I've ever tasted.'

'It's fluffy!' Rosalba agreed, chewing enthusiastically.

'But remember,' Fandango said sternly, *no more than five kilos* of popcorn kernels at a time. The neutron capacitor just *won't* take it.'

'Five kilos,' Cyril confirmed, patting the scales. 'Not a kernel more.'

Fandango spun on his Cuban heels and led the delivery men away.

At that moment Cyril's phone rang again. 'The exterminators are arriving,' he announced.

'You can deal with them,' Rosalba said. 'I'm going up to my office to choose some nice fabrics for the new curtains.'

'Come on, pals,' Salty whispered. 'Let's get a look at the enemy.'

The squirrels scurried along a cavity, emerging at a tiny spyhole right above the REX sign. It gave them a perfect view of the street outside.

Seconds later, a bright yellow van pulled up. It had the following words written on the side:

THE HONEY BADGER BROTHERS
Disposing of undesirable vermin
fairly hygienically since 2008

'Hmmm.' Salty frowned. 'This looks bad.'

Three muscular creatures bounded out of the van. Their fur was dark with a single white stripe down the back of each of their heads. Each wore a T-shirt with a single word printed on the front so that when they stood side by side they read: 'NOT SO SWEET'.

'Honey badgers!' Ben gasped. 'The toughest animals on the planet.'

'They're not even frightened of lions,' Cassie whispered.

'Gentlemen!' Cyril the manager walked out and greeted them with a trembling hand. 'Thank you for your prompt response. I've heard great things about your work.'

'I'm Gritsky,' the lead honey badger announced gruffly. 'That's Fleabilly, my second in command.'

Fleabilly saluted sharply and gave the manager a rascally wink.

'I'm Spudbasher,' said the third badger,

a toothy smile fixed on his face. He grabbed the manager's hand and spat something into his palm along with a slaver of drool. 'You can share my chewing gum if you like, mister.'

'Spuddy!' Gritsky snapped. 'Keep your chewing gum to yourself!'

'Hmmm … ' Cyril snatched his hand away, hurriedly wiping it clean with a handkerchief.

'Now,' Gritsky said. 'What's the problem?'

'Infestation,' the manager said. 'The owner thinks it's rats, but between you and me I believe we're actually talking … squirrels.'

Gritsky's eyebrows zoomed skywards.

'Squirrels?' he sniggered. He flashed a look up at the REX sign where a sudden movement had caught his eye.

'Tree-huggers!' Fleabilly scoffed.

Up behind the REX sign, Salty growled. The others curled their paws in anger.

'Rats we can respect,' Gritsky said. 'We

get a good fight out of a rat. But squirrels? Do us a favour.'

'They're quite cunning,' Cyril said.

'Cunning?' Gritsky snorted. 'Are you saying they're more cunning than US?'

'N-n-n-naturally not,' Cyril stammered. 'You are far more cunning. And strong. And brave.'

'We're not 'fraid of nothing,' Spudbasher said, pushing out his chest. 'Except I'm a bit scared of smiley clowns.'

Gritsky flicked his brother on the ear. 'Don't show weakness,' he hissed. 'I've told you that.'

'Sorry, bruv.'

'Now. When's the best moment for us to catch these losers?' Gritsky asked Cyril, taking out a small writing pad and a pencil.

'They sneak into the auditorium after the matinee,' the manager told them, 'looking for the spilled popcorn.'

Gritsky scribbled quickly. 'Time?'

'If you're back here at six thirty sharp

you'll catch them red-handed,' Cyril said.

Gritsky ripped out a page of his notepad and slipped it to the manager with a sly wink. It read: 'DON'T LOOK NOW BUT THEY'RE UP THERE BEHIND THE SIGN, LISTENING TO EVERY WORD WE SAY.'

'We'll be back,' Gritsky said. 'Six thirty on the nail. We'll storm in there with our ninja techniques.'

The three honey badgers leapt into their van and zoomed off into the city.

CHAPTER 18

STICKY SITUATIONS

Salty took his three new friends to one of his secret dens, a comfy spot in the ceiling cavity above the foyer.

The four friends chatted quietly about the adventures of the day. Then came the sound of excited families arriving for the afternoon film.

'Best popcorn ever,' came a child's voice from below.

'Awesome!' cried another.

Salty's ears pricked up. 'That's my friends down there!' he said. 'I might be able to get us a wee snack to keep us going.' Salty scampered to the gap in the ceiling and looked into the foyer.

'Psst!' he called. 'Cameron! Jasmine! Share a wee bite of popcorn with your old pal, won't you?'

Two children looked up, smiling as they saw the squirrel. 'Salty, it's you!' the girl said. 'OK, hang on a second.'

Cameron and Jasmine waited until their parents were distracted buying their tickets, then gave a thumbs up to their friend.

Salty and the others used their acrobatic skills to form a squirrel chain, dropping

down to grab the carton, then quickly clambering back up before any adults noticed.

'Thanks, pals,' Salty said with a wave.

'You're welcome!' Cameron whispered back.

The squirrels shared the treat, savouring every bite and realising it was far better than the stuff they'd eaten earlier.

'We need our own popcorn machine,' Cassie said, her eyes suddenly bright. 'That would solve our problem – and we could feed every squirrel in the city!'

'Wow!' Alfie gasped, his whiskers trembling. 'Feed *all* the hungry squirrels.'

'Great idea,' Ben agreed.

'Dream on, pals,' Salty said. 'Dream on. How would we ever get hold of our own machine?'

The squirrels finished the little snack while the film played, but their tummies were soon grumbling again with hunger. Finally they heard the music track of the credits, followed by chatter as the families left.

Salty checked the wall clock in the foyer. It was ten past six. 'Those pesky honey badgers will be here soon,' he said. 'Ben, you go on lookout. We'll collect plenty of popcorn for you.'

'OK!' Ben agreed. 'I'll watch outside for their van.'

Salty, Cassie and Alfie made their way to the gargoyle, soon looking down on the auditorium.

'There are still three people in there,' Cassie said.

'Just a few old ladies who've fallen asleep,' Salty said, waving a paw dismissively. 'That happens from time to time.'

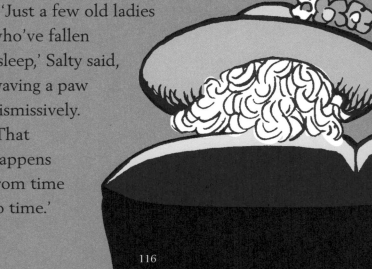

The squirrels climbed down the curtains. Their mouths began to water as they saw how much popcorn was littered on the carpet.

The three elderly ladies were fast asleep, their heads bowed down beneath extravagant flowery hats.

'They're snoring,' Alfie sniggered.

'Just ignore those old dears,' Salty said. 'Now, let's get to work before those honey badger idiots turn up. We've got fifteen minutes.'

One of the old ladies gave a particularly loud snort.

'Yes!' Cassie said. 'They blew it by announcing they'd arrive at six thirty. They had no idea we were listening in. They're not half as clever as they think.'

One of the sleeping ladies twitched her foot.

Cassie began filling up a plastic bag with popcorn for Ben. 'That doberdoodle is smarter than the honey badgers,' she said, laughing. 'And that's saying something.'

The three elderly ladies jerked in their seats.

Alfie munched happily on the popcorn, moving down the aisles. 'Stupid badgers,' he sighed. 'Squirrels more clever.'

One of the old ladies coughed in an oddly gruff way.

Alfie paused, staring at the muscular, extremely hairy leg in front of him. 'Hairy!' he sniggered. 'Hairy old lady!'

'We're the great honey badger brothers,'

Salty mimicked in a silly squeaky voice. 'We're not intelligent enough to do anything else so we chase rats and mice for money.' Salty spotted a particularly juicy piece of popcorn stuck beneath the shoe of one of the old ladies. He began, carefully, to lift the foot. 'We're so tough, we're so hard, we're the scariest creatures in the jungle, blah blah blah,' he whispered.

He reached for the popcorn. The shoe pressed down, trapping his paw.

'Ow!' Salty looked up. The three old ladies sprung to their feet, throwing off their hats.

'The honey badgers!' Cassie screamed.

'Attack!' Gritsky cried.

CHAPTER 19

AMBUSH ANTICS

Gritsky and Fleabilly flew into action, spinning through the air in a frenzy of flying fur and flashing paws. Fast as lightning they whirled, pinning down the panicking squirrels as they ran for the exit.

Spudbasher would have joined them, but couldn't. His little old lady dress was stuck in the hinge of his seat and he was too busy trying to get free.

The three squirrels were overpowered, the honey badgers used their brute strength and huge size to pin the squirrels to the floor, iron fists holding them tight. No matter how much they wriggled and fought, the honey badgers were too strong.

Two seconds later Ben popped his head round the corner. He had no sooner realised what had happened to his friends than Gritsky pounced, fast as lightning, flattening him to the ground in an instant. He too was captured. Ben's eyes darted over to his three friends, still in the claws of Fleabilly, terror in their eyes.

At that moment, Cyril arrived. 'Well done!' he cried. 'I knew I could depend on you badgers!' He pulled out his wallet and peeled off some fifty-pound notes. 'I trust this will be a suitable reward.'

Gritsky snatched the notes with a grunt.

'I'm off home now,' the manager said. 'Just pull the front door shut when you leave.

Miss Rosalba, the new owner, will lock up later.'

'What do you want us to do with *them*?' Fleabilly asked.

Cyril glared at the captive squirrels. 'Take them to the river and see if they'd like a swim!' he said.

The honey badger brothers grinned with delight.

The manager left and the brothers dragged the squirrels into the foyer of the cinema where the advertising models from the attic were lined up against the wall, ready to be thrown away.

'Looky here!' Gritsky cried.

The honey badgers stepped forward, still clutching the squirrels firmly by the arms, smiling as they inspected the old movie models.

'Look at these,' Spudbasher said, checking out the life-sized creatures in turn. 'The Abominable Snowman. Mud Monster. Red Dragon.'

'And this one,' Fleabilly added, looking at a model of a shepherd girl. She was dressed in a pretty blue dress, her face covered by a lacy bonnet.

'Little Bo Creep,' Gritsky read, raising the shepherd girl's bonnet and shivering with delight as the fibreglass face of a zombie was revealed beneath the frills.

Gritsky snapped his fingers. 'I've got an idea,' he said. 'Why don't we get a nice little photo for the website? Strap our squirrel friends to these monsters for a giggle?'

The other badgers cackled. 'Yeah,' Fleabilly agreed. 'We likes a good old piccie of our victims, we do.' He pulled a roll of sticky tape from his kitbag with his free paw.

Gritsky jostled Ben about by his arm, making him squeak. 'How about you my friend?' he said. 'What's *your* darkest fear?'

Ben's eyes flickered to the Mud Monster

as the time he had been caught in the swamp flashed into his mind.

The honey badgers grinned.

'You're going to have a little cuddle with Mr Slime, my friend,' Fleabilly cried.

'Not that,' Ben protested. 'Nooooo!'

Ben tried to pull free but the honey badger brothers quickly tied him to the Mud Monster.

'I like it,' Gritsky declared. He turned to Cassie. 'Now, what's *your* ultimate nightmare, sweetie pie?'

Cassie wriggled as hard as she could, trying to escape Fleabilly's tight grasp on her.

'Not the dragon,' Alfie called. 'The fire nearly got her in the lightning tree … '

His voice tailed away as he saw Cassie's ears flatten to her head, her lips trembling.

'Oh,' Alfie said. 'Sorry … '

'Got a thing about flames?' Gritsky leered at Cassie. 'Then I think you might enjoy the Red Dragon.'

Within seconds poor Cassie was lashed to the rubber dragon with sticky tape.

'Now you!' Gritsky snatched up Alfie and pushed him close to the Abominable Snowman's ice-encrusted face. 'It's the yeti for you!'

'Leave him!' Cassie shouted. 'It's not fair – he's too small.'

But the sticky tape whizzed into action. Alfie was taped, trembling, into the yeti's paw.

'Finally,' Gritsky announced. 'Little Bo Creep. Only one candidate for that, I think.'

Salty went pale. 'Leave it out, pal! You're not going to stick me to that *girl*, are you?' he cried, straining against Fleabilly's grip.

Gritsky and Fleabilly wrestled Salty over to Little Bo Creep. Moments later, Spudbasher had bound him tightly to the frilly skirted zombie girl.

The badgers stood back to admire their

handiwork.

'This shot will go on our home page,' Fleabilly chuckled, pulling out a camera.

'Yeah.' Gritsky nodded. 'We might even get on the cover of *Vermin Exterminator Monthly*.'

The camera flashed and the squirrels flinched. The badgers howled with laughter when they saw the shot.

'Feeling peckish now,' Gritsky said, heading towards the Pop-O-Matic 3000. 'How about we have ourselves a little snack?'

'Good plan,' Fleabilly cried. 'Time to pop!'

CHAPTER 20

MONKEY BUSINESS

The honey badgers raided the storeroom, rolling one of the huge barrels of unexploded popcorn across to the edge of the machine. They tipped the entire contents in.

'Pals! Pals!' Salty shouted, pointing at the stamp on the barrel that read 'Fifty kilos'. 'The Fandango man said not more than five kilos of unexploded popcorn at a time.'

'Really?' Fleabilly snarled. 'Well, he doesn't know about honey badger appetites.'

'The machine won't take it!' Ben cried.

'More!' Spuddy said.

'He mentioned danger to life and limb,' Cassie wailed.

'Whatever.' The honey badger brothers rolled a second barrel across. 'We're starving.'

In went another fifty kilos of the unexploded corn.

'And another,' said Gritsky.

A third huge barrel was tipped into the enormous device, then a fourth, the honey badger brothers slapping each other on their backs as they contemplated their popcorn feast.

A shriek came from the upstairs office. 'What's that row?' called Rosalba's voice. 'Who's down there? We're supposed to be closed.'

'It's just us,' Gritsky called up. 'The vermin control team.'

They heard high-heeled shoes clunking down the stairs.

'Oh-er,' Gritsky whispered. 'It's the boss.'

'She's not going to like us messing around with her film displays,' Fleabilly hissed. 'If we ever want to work here again we'd better hide them.'

The honey badger brothers leapt into action.

'Get them in there,' Gritsky crowed. He pointed at the popcorn machine.

The honey badgers swung open the huge lid at the top of the Pop-O-Matic 3000.

One by one they grabbed the four squirrel–monster bundles, the squirrels squeaking in terror as they were tossed into the machine. The badgers just had time to slam the lid shut before Rosalba swept into the foyer.

'Hello, boys!' she cried, fluttering her eyelashes at the badgers. 'Have you got rid of those *pestilential* creatures for me?'

She didn't notice the faces of the squirrels inside their poptastic prison, pressed against the glass, nor could she hear their squeaks for help through the heavy lid.

'Yes, m'lady, all gone and disposed of,' Fleabilly replied, smiling at her with

puppy-dog eyes. 'And may I say, m'lady, what a pretty sight you make in your lovely dress.'

Rosalba preened her hair, plucking at her lacquered locks.

'Why *thank you*,' she simpered. 'I do try to look my best.'

'And those, m'lady, are the sparkliest earrings I ever did see,' added Gritsky, cocking his head to one side.

Rosalba blushed deep red and fluttered her false eyelashes even faster, not noticing as one flew off. 'You are *charming*, boys,' she chimed. 'You must be hungry after all your hard work. Why don't I give you a little treat and put a couple of kilos of popcorn in the machine for you?'

She tottered towards one of the empty popcorn barrels, stopping abruptly as Fleabilly blocked her.

'We … erm … put some in the machine already,' he declared.

'Clever boys!' Rosalba cried. She spun

on her heels, crossed to the Pop-O-Matic 3000 and reached for the handle.

'Erm … a-a-actually … that m-m-might not be … ' Gritsky stammered.

Rosalba slammed down the handle. The machine began to hum, and its lights began to flash.

'Have a nice snack, boys,' she said. 'I'm going back to my office and the vital work of selecting satin cushion covers.'

Rosalba clattered up the stairs.

An ominous throbbing noise grew inside the Pop-O-Matic 3000. It vibrated gently, the vast quantity of corn shivering and hissing.

'What's happening?' Cassie cried, drowning in millions of hard little pieces of corn and trying to stay afloat.

The squirrels could feel the unexploded popcorn start to tremble and shake all around them.

CHAPTER 21

SHAKE, RATTLE AND POP

'Alfie frightened,' Alfie cried, his little bottom lip wobbling.

The squirrels tried to struggle free but the sticky tape was just too strong.

'Turn it off!' Cassie called above the vibrating sounds of the machine.

They could hear muffled speech from the honey badgers as they tried to do something.

'Where's the switch?' they heard Gritsky say. 'Try that lever.'

A clunk made the friends jump. An even louder electric hum filled the air as the machine shook faster.

'That's the super-pop handle!' came Gritsky's voice. 'You've put it into overdrive, you wally!'

'Look at the popcorn ... ' Cassie said, her eyes wide in horror.

Ben began to whimper. The hundreds of thousands of kernels around the friends were starting to glow. Tiny emerald sparks zapped from one kernel to another, the skins of each piece of corn crackling as the pressure inside them began to build.

Out in the foyer, the honey badger brothers were still scrabbling for the off switch.

'Maybe this one?' Fleabilly said. He put a furry claw on a switch then jumped back. 'Ow! It's boiling hot!' He took a step towards the door. 'You reckon we're safe here, Gritsky?'

Steam began to shoot from the control panel of the Pop-O-Matic 3000. Spudbasher moved behind Gritsky. 'Honey badgers aren't afraid of nuffin',' he said shakily.

'It's starting to look a bit dodgy,' Fleabilly said in a strangely squeaky voice.

The floor juddered beneath the machine, and the howling grew suddenly louder. The honey badger brothers clamped their paws to their ears.

Inside the machine the four friends blinked through the steam.

'If we're going to be popped,' Ben said, swallowing hard, 'at least we'll go out together. Can you get a paw free?'

Alfie and Cassie managed to wiggle an arm out of their bonds to grab Ben's paws.

'I'm scared,' Cassie sobbed.

'Alfie love you all,' Alfie said.

Cassie let out a strangled gulp.

'Salty? Will you hold paws?' Ben said.

Salty nodded. 'Aye.' He reached out and the four squirrels held each other, staring with wide, fearful eyes.

'I'm sorry for the way I behaved, pals,' Salty said slowly. 'I should have shared from the beginning.'

A blaring siren started up, announcing: 'Alert! Popping point imminent! Alert! Popping point imminent!'

A countdown screen flashed into life on the front of the machine and the voice continued:

'Ten.'

The honey badger brothers shuffled backwards a step.

'Nine.'

The control panel of the Pop-O-Matic

3000 began to glow.

'Eight.'

Rivets and bolts snapped off the gigantic machine.

'Seven.'

Rosalba called down. 'Boys? Boys? Is the Pop-O-Matic all right?'

'Six.'

A panel fell away, revealing the red-hot guts of the machine.

Rosalba called down again. 'What on earth is that extraordinary noise?'

'Five.'

The glass dome of a nearby gobstopper vending machine suddenly cracked. Rainbow-coloured gobstoppers bounced across the foyer.

'OW!' Fleabilly yelled as one of the rock-hard sweets thumped his big toe.

'Four.'

The Pop-O-Matic 3000 began to blare out: 'WARNING! POPCORN OVERLOAD! WARNING! POPCORN

OVERLOAD!'

Fleabilly and Spudbasher looked to Gritsky, panic in their eyes.

'Three.'

The speakers got louder: 'STAND BACK! DANGER! STAND BACK! DANGER! POPCORN LOADING EXCEEDS MANUFACTURER'S RECOMMENDATIONS!'

The honey badger brothers ran for their lives.

'Two.'

'EVACUATE! EVACUATE!'

'One.'

The frantic yells from the speakers were suddenly replaced with a calm female voice announcing: 'The manufacturers of the Pop-O-Matic 3000 accept no legal liability for structural damage, personal injury or death.'

POPOFF!

CHAPTER 22

THE BIG BANG

Meanwhile, 5,400 miles away, in an earthquake-spotting centre in San Diego, USA, an inky needle started jerking as if it had been seized by a crazy spider.

A technician hurriedly ripped out the graph it had made. 'The big one!' he yelled, looking at the wiggly line on the paper. 'The San Andreas fault has popped off!'

'That ain't no earthquake buddy,' his colleague said, his mouth dropping open as he stared at the chart. 'That's an explosion on the other side of the *world*. Must have been one monster of a bang.'

Back in the epicentre of the blast it was raining popcorn. The popcorn poured down like the most intense hailstorm,

for miles around, sending bewildered citizens staggering into the streets, their eardrums throbbing. They stared wide-eyed at the popcorn that fell from the heavens, pinching themselves to make sure they weren't dreaming.

And what of the cinema? Hardly a molecule remained. The flashing REX sign was later found to have travelled 103 miles, crashing through the roof of Buckingham Palace and coming to rest on the queen's bed.

Within the popcorn fallout zone, children ran out of their classrooms, crying with delight as they stood beneath the falling popcorn.

'Caramel!' they cried, gathering up handfuls from the playground and crunching on the sweet treat.

'Children, NO!' their teachers cried. 'It's probably got a lurgy! Don't eat it!'

'Butter!' They swallowed it as fast as they could shovel it down. 'Salty!'

One boy screwed up his face in disappointment. 'Plain!' he said in disgust. 'Yuck!' He spat the piece out.

Back at the blast site, the honey badger brothers were dusting themselves down as the popcorn continued to fall from the skies.

'I think we might have overdone it a bit,' Fleabilly gulped.

The Pop-O-Matic 3000 had vaporised. Vanished. Vamoosed. In its place was a mysterious mass – perhaps the weirdest wobbly wonder that's ever been seen.

Scientists gave it a special name: an Überpop.

It looked like a mega-mongous piece of popcorn. Eight metres wide and five metres high, its surface was as thick and bouncy as the

scummy skin on a bowl of school custard,
its shape rather like a colossal conker,
nicely rounded with crinkly bits.

The honey badger brothers moved
cautiously in. They sniffed at the skin.

'It smells sweet,' Fleabilly said.

'But also musty,' Gritsky added with a frown. 'Like a mouldy banana.'

'Popcorn to last a lifetime,' Fleabilly said with a smile. 'I'm going to try it.'

He lunged forward, his jaws wide. Gritsky pulled him back, his eyes glittering. 'No,' he said, rubbing his paws. 'No munching! We can sell this to someone – make a fortune.'

The Überpop trembled. The honey badgers stepped back as a curious, muffled noise came from within.

The brothers gasped. A crack had appeared in the skin of the Überpop.

'It's splitting,' Spudbasher said.

'Hatching like … like an egg,' Gritsky added uneasily.

'You don't think there's … something … inside, do you?' Fleabilly whispered.

'There can't be,' Gritsky said. 'C-c-c-c-can there?'

CHAPTER 23

THE STRANGE AFFAIR OF THE ÜBERPOP

The surface of the giant popcorn shook. The little crack widened, revealing a spooky darkness inside. Luminous green smoke puffed out of the gap.

'You don't think it's … alive?' Fleabilly gulped.

The Überpop rocked from side to side. A bump appeared, rising like a bubble in a pan of porridge, then quickly vanishing again.

A muffled squeak could be heard. Then a couple of high-pitched grunts. The honey badger brothers glanced at each other.

'There's *something* in there,' Spudbasher muttered, clasping Gritsky's paw, 'and it sounds a lickle bit cross.'

A scaly claw sliced through the skin of the Überpop.

Fleabilly stepped back. 'Something's going to be born.'

'And it ain't no baby,' Gritsky said.

A bright red, fluffy head emerged. It was a super-sized, super-red version of Cassie, with the same melting eyes and shiny nose, but with the addition of a series of dragon spikes down the back of her head. Seconds later, the body shot out with the sort of *pop* only normally heard when a large pin is stuck in a gigantic balloon.

'It's half squirrel, half dragon!' Gritsky exclaimed.

'A squagon!' Fleabilly whispered.

The gargantuan Cassie stood on her rear legs, three times the height of a man.

'It's the girl!' Fleabilly said. 'She's got mixed up with the dragon in the popcorn meltdown incident and become a kind of squirrel–dragon superhero mutant monster thingy.'

Cassie looked down at her body, her
expression one of utter amazement. 'I'm
a dragon!' she realised. 'What fun!'

She made a sudden flapping movement,
revealing two enormous dragon wings
that crackled as they unfurled.

'Wings … ' said Cassie, astonished.
'Cool!' She tried an experimental flap,

taking off clumsily and crashing like a dizzy duck after a few seconds. 'Whoops!'

'Don't worry, bruvs,' Gritsky said. 'It might look a bit dangerous but I don't think it can actually DO anything.'

Cassie's expression changed. She twitched. 'I'm going to sn—' She clutched at her nose. 'I'm going to sn … sn … sn … Achoo!'

She sneezed, letting rip with a breathy blast of fire. The flame shot out from her mouth, missing the honey badgers by a whisker.

'Gosh!' Cassie giggled.

'It r-r-r-r-really is a dragon,' Fleabilly stammered. 'Can we handle a d-d-d-d-dragon in a fight?'

'Honey badgers fear nothing,' Gritsky reminded him. 'We're unbeatable.'

The Überpop rocked again. A second pair of paws slithered free – paws covered in a gunky green substance that looked suspiciously like slime.

'Half squirrel, half slime monster.'
Fleabilly shivered. 'It's disgusting.'

The new arrival slipped out of the Über-pop and stood up, a full five metres tall.

'Ben?' Cassie said. 'Is that you? You're a … a … a gunk creature!'

Ben examined himself, a mischievous grin creeping across his face. 'So I am!' he cried. He clapped his paws together, creating a massive slime pie that splatted on to the ground. 'Wow!' he said. 'I can do goo.'

'Very clever,' Gritsky scoffed. 'We'll soon teach you a lesson.'

Gritsky and his brothers ran at the gunky squirrel, but Ben was ready for them. He pushed out his paws, sending a stream of slippery, green gloop flying through the air. It bowled the honey badgers off their feet, coating them from head to toe.

'Steady on,' Fleabilly spluttered. 'That's not fair.'

'We can beat them,' Gritsky said, clearing slime from his ears. 'We're … still … not … scared.'

The Überpop shivered. An icy blast shot out of the gap. Seconds later, Alfie emerged – a mighty snow-squirrel with shaggy white fur and dagger-like icicles dangling from his nose.

'Half yeti, half squirrel,' Fleabilly said, staring up at him.

'A squeti,' Spudbasher added.

'Bbbbbrrrrrrr!' Alfie cried. 'Alfie freeeeeeezing.'

'You're allowed to be freezing. You're an ice monster,' Cassie said. She patted him on the back, then removed her hand quickly when it started to freeze to Alfie's white fur.

'What's your trick, Mr Yeti Monster?' Gritsky said sarcastically. 'Snowball windy bottoms?'

The other badgers cackled with laughter.

Alfie clutched at his belly. 'Alfie tummy

feels funny.'

The smiles froze on the honey badgers' faces.

'Alfie botty gone chilly.'

The honey badgers took a step back, their faces turning as pale as curdled milk.

Alfie spun around, his monstrous ice-coated tail beginning to rise.

CHAPTER 24

ALFIE'S REVENGE

Three snowballs popped at high speed from Alfie's backside, each the size of a beach ball.

SPLODGE!

SPLODGE!

SPLODGE!

They slammed into the horrified badgers, instantly burying each of them in their own personal avalanche. Three mounds of snow wobbled and shook.

One by one, the honey badgers dug themselves free.

'Th-th-this is beyond a joke,' Gritsky protested, his teeth chattering with the cold.

Spudbasher cleared snow from his ears and blinked ice crystals from his eyes. 'Can I go home now, please?' he said with a shiver.

'No!' Gritsky snapped. 'Just because these squirrels have turned into superheroes doesn't mean we quit!'

'Yeah. What about the fat one?' Fleabilly taunted. 'Is he gonna turn into a *superhero* as well? Are we gonna have to run for our lives from old tubby?'

'Good point, bro,' Gritsky chimed in, his voice dripping with scorn. 'You think that lardy squirrel can scare the honey badger brothers? I mean, *please*!'

A new noise ripped through the air. The Überpop began to vibrate as a growly Scottish voice began to sing …

'Some little girls
Like ribbons and curls
And kissing their dollies goodnight.
But Little Bo Creep
Will make you weep
So you'd better look out for a fright!'

A stomach-curdling scream was followed by, 'Here's *Salty*!' as a three-metre-high creature exploded from the Überpop.

There was an awkward pause and the world stood still as the others stared at Salty.

'Erm …' Ben said.

'What?' replied Salty.

'You're wearing a dress!' Gritsky smirked.

'Yeah! A pretty little outfit!' Fleabilly taunted.

Salty screwed up his eyes and took a stumbling step towards the honey badger brothers. 'Are you calling me *girly?*' he snarled. He jabbed his paw at the badgers. 'I'm *Salty* the superhero!'

He strutted back and forth, slapping his chest and brandishing his shepherd's crook as if it were an axe.

'I'm a macho superhero, pals, and you'd better believe it!'

'Erm, it's true, Salty,' Ben told him kindly. 'You're a girl. Well, you're dressed as a girl.'

'Girly, girly, girly!' Alfie sang.

Salty stopped mid-stride. He looked slowly down at his uniform, his eyes bulging as he saw the pretty blue dress, the frilly bloomers beneath and the dainty bow around his waist.

'You're Little Bo Creep!' Gritsky said, laughing.

Salty fumed, his teeth grinding as he realised what had happened.

'Where's your sheep, little *girl*?' Fleabilly teased.

'Baaaa! Baaaa!' bleeted Spudbasher.

'Give us a kiss, sweetheart.' Fleabilly puckered up his lips.

Salty turned towards the badgers, his bloodshot eyes fixing them with a terrible glare.

'I'll give you a kiss all right,' he said slowly, clenching his paw into a fist.
'A kiss from north of the border, pal.
A kiss you'll never forget!'

'You'd better scram,' Ben told the badgers. 'While you still can.'

'Yes,' added Cassie. 'Get out of here and never come back.'

'We … ' Alfie added, linking arms with the others, 'are the Popcorn-Eating Squirrels!'

The brothers scowled. 'Honey badgers don't yield to man nor beast!' Fleabilly cried. 'We took on the job to get rid of you squirrels and that's what we're going to do.'

'Come on, badgers,' Gritsky yelled. 'Get them!'

CHAPTER 25

SNOW BUSINESS

'This'll teach you!' Fleabilly cried. He picked up a big handful of snow, shaped it into a snowball and threw it directly at Salty.

Cassie opened her mouth, shooting a jet of dragon fire into the path of the snowball, melting it immediately.

'Oh,' Fleabilly said. 'Drat!'

'*Haaaiiii-YAH!*' Gritsky screamed. He spun once, twice, building up speed and launching himself into a spectacular ninja kick jump.

He hit Ben full on the chest but the result wasn't what he expected. The honey badger's foot merely squelched into Ben's slimy green body.

Gritsky wriggled. His foot stayed stuck.

'Yuck!' he said. 'Can I have my foot back, please?'

Ben roared a battle cry right at Gritsky's head, coating him with goo, then swatted him to the ground.

'I'll get you mutants!' Fleabilly charged at them, but Alfie quickly shot a brace of spinning snowballs at the frenzied badger, blasting him with freezing snow. Fleabilly tumbled backwards.

'Ow!'

Salty joined in the combat with his shepherd's crook, whirling it at the badgers as they tried to attack. The brothers were quickly outwrestled by the towering superpowered monster squirrels.

'What shall we do with them?' Cassie wondered aloud as she looked at the exhausted badgers lying defeated on the ground.

Ben looked around and spotted the empty popcorn barrels stuck in the bare branches of a nearby tree, blown there by the explosion. He walked over and found a surprise: clinging to the same tree was the quivering, dazed form of Rosalba.

'I used to be an actress, you know … an actress.' She grinned groggily at Ben, her normal dazzling smile now quite a lot less dazzling since her false teeth had been blown out in the blast.

Ben snatched her down.

'Thank you *so* much,' Rosalba said, still dazed and confused. 'I've always relied on the kindness of … strangers.'

'Fellow squirrels,' Ben announced as he hoisted the empty barrels down, 'I've got an idea. Give me a hand.' He nodded to the three honey badgers, and the squirrels knew exactly what to do.

They grabbed the brothers, kicking and screaming, and stuffed them inside the empty popcorn barrels, sealing the lids.

'We were only following orders!' Gritsky said, his voice muffled inside the barrel.

'Tell it to the mermaids!' Ben said.

'Mermaids?' Gritsky replied, his voice shaky. He rapped on the metal wall of the drum. 'What are you going to do with us? What mermaids? Hey!'

Rosalba was stumbling around the popcorn blast site. 'Where's my cinema? What have you done with it?'

Her expression darkened. She fell to her knees.

'Gone!' she wailed. 'All gone!'

Her head snapped up. She pointed her sharpened nails at the squirrel superheroes. 'I bet this is your fault,' she hissed, her face twisted with hatred. 'You stupid, evil, supersized creatures! I'll get my revenge! I'll have you hunted down and sent far, far away! No matter the cost! You're finished! I'll—'

Ben and Cassie gripped Rosalba and stuffed her in the fourth barrel.

'What the blazes!' she shrieked.

They snapped the lid shut.

'You can't do this to ME!' Rosalba shrilled. 'The mayor is a personal friend. Don't you know who I AM?'

'Follow me, team!' Ben told his friends, tucking Rosalba's barrel under his arm. The three others began rolling the other barrels along the stony ground.

'Ow! Oooh! Ow!' the honey badger brothers yelled as they rolled over and over, moaning and groaning every second of the way.

The squirrels trundled their prisoners across the empty road, through the deserted shopping mall and into the market square.

The government had evacuated the city but there were still a few dazed humans around. They ran for their lives when they saw the squirrel superheroes lumbering towards them.

Finally the squirrels reached the banks of the fast-flowing river that ran right through the centre of the city.

'OK,' Ben said. 'Take off the lids.'

CHAPTER 26

LIFE ON THE OCEAN WAVE

The squirrel superheroes flipped off the tops of the barrels. The honey badger brothers looked out, scowling. Rosalba popped her head up, dizzy and confused.

'You going to let us free?' Gritsky said. He twisted his face into something that was – almost – a smile. 'We're quite nice really.'

'Definitely,' Ben exclaimed. 'You will be free as … fish.'

'Push!' Salty cried.

The superhero squirrels thrust the four barrels out into the churning river.

'In a couple of miles you'll reach the sea!' Ben told them. 'Bon voyage!'

'Been nice knowing you!' Salty cried.

'I've got a game of bridge at six,' Rosalba whimpered.

Alfie frowned. 'Alfie worried,' he said. 'Where will they go?'

'Don't worry,' Ben replied with a wink. 'It's just to teach them a lesson. There are plenty of ships out there. They'll bob around for a while and get picked up in no time.'

The honey badger brothers and Rosalba were swept, yabbering and screaming, round a bend in the river and out of view.

Cassie stared at her reflection in the water. 'We really are monsters,' she said sadly.

'Alfie like this for ever?' Alfie asked.

'I can't bear it,' Cassie said. 'I don't want to be a dragon. I want to be a squirrel again. Just a normal squirrel.'

'Me too,' Ben agreed.

'We have to change back,' Salty said. 'The question is, *how?*'

Just then they heard the clattering roar of helicopters and the crunch of countless pairs of boots marching in step down the road.

The crackle of a megaphone blared out. 'Attention! All abnormally large squirrel-based life forms! You are under arrest! Come forward peacefully with your ha— I mean *paws* in the air!'

'What can we do?' Cassie asked. 'We're too big to hide.'

The *clump, clump, clump* of the soldiers' boots came ever closer. The squirrels were just a few marching steps from discovery.

The four friends looked around.

'We can't even hide in the trees,' Ben gulped. 'There are only the tree trunks left.'

Cassie smiled. 'We can't hide *in* the trees,' she said. 'But maybe we can *be* the trees. Let me try …'

She climbed up the nearest bare trunk, curling her gigantic fluffy tail around her in the most ingenious way so that nothing could be seen of her body and head.

She was shaped like a tree. A fuzzy reddy-grey tree.

Ben clapped his hands. 'Great plan!' he cried.

The others jumped for the nearest tree trunks, climbing up and arranging themselves in the same way.

Seconds later the soldiers arrived.

'Halt!' cried the commander.

The soldiers stopped. Curled up on the trees, the four giant squirrels each held their breath, fearing discovery at any moment.

'We're getting reports the monsters are *extremely* close,' said the commander, strutting about right beneath the squirrels. 'Look out for mutated squirrels of the giant variety.'

The soldiers glanced around them.

'You can't miss them,' the commander said. 'Squirrels that humungous can run but they can't hide. They're just too big.' He moved a few steps and placed his hand on the trunk of Salty's tree. 'Only a buffoon could fail to spot them,' he crowed. 'Are you buffoons, men?'

'Sir, no, sir!' the men yelled.

'Only the densest type of dunce could miss them,' he continued. 'Are you dense dunces, men?'

'Sir, no, sir!'

'The government wants them captured,' he told them. 'There are experiments to be run on them, laboratory tests …'

Alfie shivered, uttering a tiny squeak.

A big ball of snow fell from him, splatting on the ground.

'What the … ?' The commander stared at Alfie's tree for a moment, then stepped towards the snowball, his face creased with suspicion.

CHAPTER 27

FANDANGO ON THE SPOT

'Commander!' came a dazed voice from behind. 'It is I – Fandango! Did you say something about mutated squirrels?'

The commander spun round. The smart-suited inventor and former magician was stumbling around the rubble, staring at the devastation in horror.

'They must have climbed into my machine,' he mumbled. 'My beloved Pop-O-Matic 3000.'

The commander frowned at him.

Fandango was sweaty and hot, his shirt collar stained with orange from his streaky fake tan.

'I know you,' the commander said. 'You're the one with that rabbit – the one that was all over the news—'

'Enough about the rabbit!' Fandango said, his voice squeaking with fury. 'Besides, don't you think there are more important things to talk about? Such as my machine creating these pesky mega-squirrels?'

'If your machine did this, you are in big trouble,' the commander barked. 'Creating massive squirrel monsters is against the law.'

Fandango fell to his knees, his face crumpling. 'I'm sorry!' the inventor blustered. 'I did tell them not to put more than five kilos of—'

The commander yanked him back to his feet. 'Think, man, think! You say your machine caused this mutation, so surely it can be reversed?'

Fandango loosened his cravat and gulped down air. 'It's hopeless!' he wailed. 'The neutron capacitor just isn't up to it.'

'The nation is relying on you, man! What if they *breed*?'

'Wait!' Fandango snapped his fingers. 'I've just realised something! Let me think … '

Fandango paced back and forth, clutching his head in his hands. Then he turned back to the commander.

'There's only one machine that can solve this problem,' he said gravely.

'Yes? What is it?' The commander grabbed Fandango by the lapels. 'Spit it out, man, spit it out!'

'A candyfloss machine the size of a house,' Fandango said, raising his arms triumphantly. 'With a rotational vortex in the sugar-spinning drum of ninety-nine-point-seven per cent of the speed of light.'

The commander slumped back. 'Well that's a fat lot of use,' he moaned. 'Such a thing obviously doesn't exist. Only a madman would make a machine like that.'

'Indeed …' Fandango said with a curious smile. 'Catch those squirrels, sir, and bring them to my workshop! There's no time to lose!'

One of the soldiers suddenly pointed at the nearby trees. 'Sir! Those trees,' he yelled. 'They're not trees at all. It's the gigantic, evil squirrel monsters!'

The furry trees exploded into life, the soldiers scattering in terror as the squirrels leapt to the ground.

The squirrels sprinted through the popcorn-laden streets, hundreds of soldiers on their trail. Buildings and shops whizzed past in a blur as they ran.

'We have to find Fandango's workshop,' Ben puffed. 'You heard what he said about the giant candyfloss machine, it could change us back to normal!'

'There's his van!' Cassie pointed to the right. They slowed down as they saw a rainbow-coloured vehicle painted with Fandango's grinning face and the words:

FANDANGO FABRICATIONS LTD
Unfeasibly large confectionery machines are our speciality!
Come and see our showroom at 44 Einstein Street

'Einstein Street – that's where we need to go,' Ben said, speeding up again.

'HALT! Stop immediately,' blasted a megaphone behind them. 'Resistance is useless.'

'They're gaining on us!' Cassie cried.

CHAPTER 28

CANDYFLOSS CHAOS

The squirrels dashed down a deserted street. Salty was lagging behind. The noise of thumping military boots seemed to be getting closer and closer.

'Faster, Salty! Faster!' Ben yelled.

'You try running in a dress, pal,' Salty wheezed. 'These bloomers are chafing me like crazy.'

They came to a junction. Cassie looked left. Ben looked right. The streets were unfamiliar. They had no idea which way to go.

'Lost!' Alfie exclaimed.

The clunking rattle of tanks reached their ears.

Then they saw movement. Two children came round the corner, gathering up

popcorn and stuffing it in their pockets.

'Jasmine! Cameron!' Salty cried. 'It's me!'

The two children froze on the spot, their mouths wide open as they stared up at the squirrel superheroes.

'Salty?' Jasmine said slowly.

'You've gone all big,' Cameron added with a gulp.

'And you're wearing … frilly … girly knickers,' Jasmine said doubtfully. 'Why?'

'Never mind about that!' Salty snapped. 'We need your help. D'you know where Einstein Street is?'

The two children looked at each other.

'Erm … yes,' Jasmine said.

'Can you show us the way?'

'Give us a piggyback and it's a deal,' Cameron said.

Salty scooped up Cameron, placing him on his shoulders, and Cassie did the same with Jasmine.

'Whoooo!' Jasmine shrieked, clinging to

Cassie's ears for dear life as she pounded the streets. 'Left here! Then left again!'

'Right here!' said Cameron, his eyes shining at the thrilling ride. At a couple of junctions the superheroes created mud and snow barricades to delay the troops. Gradually the soldiers fell further back.

Ten minutes later they came to an industrial area.

'Here's Einstein Street,' Jasmine announced.

The squirrels slowed a little, looking for number forty-four. 'Don't slow down too much!' cried Ben, 'we don't know how much time we've got.'

Jasmine and Cameron kept their eyes peeled behind them, checking for any sign of the soldiers, while the squirrels counted the houses.

'Thirty-eight, forty, forty-two ... forty-four! This must be it!' exclaimed Cassie, as they all came to halt outside a square, towering building.

They burst in through the door of the giant warehouse, into a huge space filled to the brim with bizarre-looking contraptions.

'Where's the candyfloss machine?' Ben puffed.

'Over here,' Salty cried. He was standing

by the biggest invention of all, a shiny red structure roughly the size of a house.

A control panel on the side glowed with illuminated buttons.

'Press the on switch when we tell you,' Cassie told Jasmine and Cameron.

The squirrels pushed through a hatch to enter the machine. They walked past gleaming brass cogs, reaching the inside of a polished metal drum that stretched as high as the ceiling, easily big enough to take the four friends.

'Awesome!' Ben exclaimed.

Above them was a clear plastic container filled with tons and tons of bright pink sugar.

Cassie saw a sign and read it aloud: 'Warning! Candyfloss Flossing Zone. Do not operate at more than ninety-five per cent of the speed of light.'

'Fandango said ninety-nine point seven,' Salty said.

'We have to take the chance,' Cassie said.

'Come on. Stand against the wall and spread your arms and legs out.'

'OK, kids!' Salty cried. 'Go for it.'

'Pressing the button now,' Jasmine called.

A shrill siren blasted and the cylinder began to turn.

'Here we go,' Cassie said. The four friends leant back, their hearts beating fast as the machine accelerated from zero to fifty revolutions a minute in the blink of an eye.

'Alfie tummy!' Alfie yelled, a huge smile on his face. 'Getting left behind! It's cool!'

The speed increased, pinning the squirrels to the wall like motorcycle riders in a wall of death. Above them, the drum of pink sugar began to jiggle. Sugar cascaded down like a pink Niagara Falls. The candyfloss contraption clicked up a few gears and the four friends found their vision beginning to blur.

Salty moaned. 'Here I go again!'

The first strands of sticky pink candyfloss began to zap through the air. The squirrels blinked as the wispy floss stuck to their fur, collected on their noses and settled on the tips of their ears.

'I've got candyfloss eyelashes!' Cassie called.

'We're going pink,' shouted Alfie. 'It's awesome!'

'Look at that,' Salty cried.

The LED screen was flickering like disco lights. Sixty. Seventy. Eighty per cent of the speed of light. Ninety. With every

passing second the whirling drum was
getting closer to warp speed.

'Like being in a sugar cloud!' Ben called.

'I'm breathing candyfloss!' Cassie added.

'Ninety-nine per cent!' Salty said with
a strangled cry.

There came a humungous …

SPLAT!

Then everything went …
Pink.

CHAPTER 29

THAT SHRINKING FEELING

The army had arrived in Einstein Street. Amongst them, a wild-eyed Fandango stumbled forward, falling to his knees and beating at the ground.

'My workshop,' he sobbed. 'What have they done?'

The inventor's workplace was indeed a startling sight, since the roof had been blown away by a soaring column of candyfloss. Fandango craned his neck, peering into the stratosphere, blinking away his tears.

'Lost in the clouds,' he spluttered. 'I can't even see the top.'

Then his eyes widened as he saw the candyfloss had a particular shape ... the shape of two massive rabbit ears.

'Rabbit ears!' Fandango wept. 'The curse of the rabbit has finally struck! He'll haunt me to my last days on earth!'

Fandango hopped down the road like a frazzled bunny and disappeared round the corner.

'Sir! I see movement!' called a soldier.

The door to Fandango's workshop opened a crack. The soldiers shifted nervously.

'Come out with your hands up!' the commander yelled.

Jasmine and Cameron stared uncertainly at the soldiers, then slowly walked out, each holding two huge sticks of bright pink candyfloss.

'What are you children doing here?' the commander asked, narrowing his eyes. 'Have you seen four massive squirrel monster thingies?'

'They've gone,' Jasmine said innocently.

'What about small squirrels? Tell the truth.'

'There's not a single squirrel in that building,' Cameron said. He took a mouthful of the pink confectionery and chewed it slowly.

A rather bad-tempered Scottish voice whispered from inside the candyfloss, 'Watch out for my tail, pal.'

Jasmine and Cameron walked calmly towards Blackwater Park, the squirrels safely hidden inside the candyfloss they were carrying.

When they reached the pond Jasmine called, 'All clear,' and the four friends pushed their way out of their sticky cocoons.

'We did it,' Cassie exclaimed. 'Fandango's candyfloss machine worked!'

The squirrels embraced.

'You're completely pink!' Cameron smiled. 'Candyfloss squirrels.'

Cassie and the others bounded to the water's edge, quickly washing their fur clean.

Cassie looked at Ben. 'You used to be scared of the pond,' she said. 'Scared of the mud.'

Ben looked surprised. 'You're right,' he said, staring at the marshy area where he had once been trapped. 'I suppose when you've been a slime monster, it's not frightening any more.'

Cassie looked at the lightning tree, the charred remains of which had always struck terror into her heart.

The feeling of panic had gone.

'Same for me,' she said, smiling proudly.

Thunder rumbled. The sky darkened. Rain began to fall. The squirrels and children ran to the bandstand to get some cover.

'How about you, Alfie?' Cassie asked kindly.

'What?'

'You still frightened of ice and snow?'

'Ice is nice!' Alfie said, puffing out his chest. 'Alfie is the snow monster!'

The friends chatted as the storm gradually eased off. Then something beeped in Cameron's pocket. He quickly checked his mobile.

'That's Mum – she's wondering where we are,' he said.

CHAPTER 30

SWEET PARTINGS AND NEW BEGINNINGS

'You'd better get home,' Cassie told the children. 'Thanks for all your help.'

'It's been cool,' Cameron said with a smile. 'Can we do it again?'

The squirrels laughed out loud.

'Forget it, pal,' Salty said. 'It's the quiet life for us from now on.'

Jasmine and Cameron said goodbye and ran off.

The squirrels walked to the edge of the park, popcorn squishing soggily beneath their feet.

They stopped by the road.

'Well?' Cassie said. 'What next?'

'We can stay here,' Alfie said. 'There's popcorn everywhere.'

He stuffed a pawful of popcorn into his mouth, then spat it back out with a disgusted expression.

'Soggy!' he said. 'Gooey! Slimy! Yuck!'

'The rain has ruined it already,' Cassie said.

'You don't know any more cinemas do you?' Ben asked Salty.

Salty laughed. 'That's exactly what I was thinking, young laddie. We need *fresh* popcorn and that's why *that* poster is a sight for sore eyes.'

Salty pointed ahead to a brightly lit advertising billboard. On it was a giant, glamorous cruise ship, sailing into a setting sun.

The advert said:

> **Esmerelda Cruise Lines**
> invites you to join us on the
> inaugural round-the-
> world voyage of the brand-new
> ## Esmerelda Exotica!
> Three swimming pools. Climbing wall.
> Six-screen multiplex cinema.

'It's the ship Fandango spoke about,' Salty said. 'He said he'd installed a Pop-O-Matic 3000 on board.'

Salty climbed up the billboard, followed by the others.

Perched on the top, they had a good view of the city. There in the distance, poking above the skyline, was a gleaming white ship.

'The *Esmerelda Exotica*!' Alfie exclaimed.

'A whole multiplex,' Salty said. 'Six screens. Hundreds of kids on board. Can you *imagine* how much dropped popcorn there will be with SIX screens?'

'Wait. What's that smell?' Ben said.

The squirrels raised their heads, sniffing the air as a glorious aroma wafted across the city.

'The sweetness!' Cassie cried.

'They're testing the Pop-O-Matic 3000.' Salty's eyes gleamed. 'Ready for the first voyage.' He rubbed his tummy.

'I think we've just found our new home,' Ben said. 'Can you get us there, Salty?'

'Oh, aye,' Salty said. 'I do believe I can. There's not a second to lose. It could be launching at any minute.'

A firework burst into the sky above the cruise ship.

Cassie turned to Ben and Alfie. 'We

might never see the park again,' she said. 'You know that, don't you?'

'It's OK,' Ben said slowly. 'It's time for new adventures.'

'Maybe we'll even make that idea I had come true,' Cassie added. 'One day we'll get a machine of our own so we can make popcorn for ALL the hungry squirrels!'

'Great plan!' Alfie exclaimed. 'Fresh popcorn for everyone!'

'Come on!' Salty called. 'Let's go!'

Alfie, Ben and Cassie took a last, lingering look at the park. Then they scampered down the billboard and followed Salty into the night.

THE END

About the Author

Matt Dickinson is a writer and filmmaker with a passion for climbing and adventure. A father of five children, his proudest climbing achievement is standing on the summit of Mount Everest. Matt is passionate about children's education, and tours primary schools across the UK and abroad. Matt talks about the inspiration for his books, reading aloud and nurturing a love of reading and adventure in even the most reluctant pupil. Engaging creative writing sessions can also be scheduled, and Matt will share pictures from his Everest expeditions – the inspiration for the second book in this series, *Popcorn-Eating Squirrels: Lost on Everest!* If you would like a school visit from Matt please contact him: *www.mattdickinson.com*